THE FIFTH GUARDIAN

A SYMPHONY OF DISCORD

Barry M. Fellinger

And I would choose you,
in a hundred lifetimes,
in a hundred worlds.
In any version of reality,
I would find you and I'd choose you.

For Lindsay

Dedicated to all those whose lived experiences of unexpected tragedy and loss have made them believe that perhaps the universe is not always unfolding as it should…

Prelude

A musical section or movement introducing the theme or chief subject (as of a fugue or suite) or serving as an introduction to an opera or oratorio.

Prelude: Guardians

At the Crossroads where the origin points of Space and Time intersect with those of Eternity and Infinity, the Four Guardians hold in place. For untold millennia they have been there. Aloof. Steadfast. Silent Sentinels. Vigilant protectors of The All.

They exist, often motionless, consistently genderless, even the memories of their own origins of how they came to be, lost across the vast oceans of time. Neither fully omniscient nor fully omnipresent, yet they know much and see much, for an extremely high level of cosmic perception is theirs. They do not know all, nor are they able to traverse the flow states of Time, limited still to only The Now.

Their mission: to Guard The All, from any and all threats, within and without. The Guardians are ever ready to stand against and protect the fragile balance at the entrance ways of the thresholds to the Primal Forces of Infinity, Eternity, Time and Space. All interconnected, yet separate, they keep all that is, as it should be. All joined, yet each to their own purpose. They guard against anything that would disrupt the Harmony that is The All.

The Guardians exist as both corporeal and non-corporeal entities depending on need. Their density, when corporeal, so full that they pass through matter as most sentients would walk through air. With thoughts interconnected, they can turn them, singly or collectively, to reach out, search and view within and across The All, as need arises. Most times, passive observers, rarely intervenors.

They do possess the ability to appear in corporeal form to the vast array of creatures and sentients who live, move and experience being across and within The All. Those are rare occurrences and seldom do the Guardians engage in such, except in dire need. Regardless, all creatures, including the sentient beings who populate The All, have no concept of the Guardians, nor could most grasp even the simplest aspect of their being without their minds collapsing.

The Four Guardians hold in place at the Nexus.

PART I

Harmony

In music, harmony is the process by which individual sounds are joined together or composed into whole units or compositions. Often, the term harmony refers to simultaneously occurring frequencies, pitches or chords.

The little girl has been walking for a long time, yet she is not hungry or thirsty. She does not know why. She just is not. She keeps walking.

CHAPTER ONE

Da Capo

Da Capo is a musical term that means "from the beginning."

Lindsay – Nightfall

Sixty-six universes over from its first iteration, and 1,986 galaxies in, on the inner edge of the Orion Arm, in one of the four spiral arms within a solar system whose third planet from the sun boasts a billion plus sentient lifeforms, a young father holds a prematurely newborn infant in his arms as she struggles to breathe, fighting for life. Except for the tears, his wife remains quiet, feeling both fear and anguish as she lies in her hospital bed after having just delivered. It was too early.

This backwater mud ball, as the father sometimes calls it, does not possess the medical technology necessary to intervene and save the baby's life. Perhaps two or three decades later it will exist. But not now. Too soon. Too late. The father, tears running down his face, dedicates his baby daughter to the God he thought he knew. His wife remains too angry to cry or to believe in this moment. Too much emotion. Too many questions. Too few answers.

Knowing her life will soon end, the father lets his wife hold the dying infant one more time before they return her to the nurses. They cannot bear to see her last moments. Their time too brief. This is too much. Not enough. The whole scene feels surreal, the evening lighting of hospital corridors and rooms only adding to their sense of distortion, disbelief and detachment as they experience both life and death so eerily proximate.

They name the baby Lindsay Marie Hope. At least they have that much: a name by which to remember their first daughter. Hope springs eternal, after all. Still, all seems hopeless. They had such dreams for her, believed she would do something significant, something special for their world. Something truly unique.

THE FIFTH GUARDIAN: A SYMPHONY OF DISCORD

The young couple grieves. A malevolence observes.
A Guardian weeps. A thread ends.

Interlude - The All

The All. It is simply that: The All, The Everything, The All-Encompassing. All.

Those sentients among the more evolved races intelligent enough to grasp the basic concept, have varying names for it. Words such as Omniverse, Ultraverse and Multiverse allow a basic, limited level of comprehension. Truly though, their terms fall far short of attempting to describe the true nature of The All.

Certain civilizations with deeper advanced languages where words may have multiple meanings, could go a bit beyond scratching the surface of the concept of The All. Even then, deep words with many meanings only go so far before they too, fail. Eventually language, regardless of how advanced or how precise, is limited and unable to reveal or express the true nature and meaning of The All.

Those species within The All who came into existence as forms of energy, or races evolved to that higher state of untethered consciousness are probably the only beings that can come close to truly comprehending The All, particularly the ones able to communicate without words, using only the energy of thought to convey meaning. Those are rare; even across the infinite number of worlds The All holds, these higher beings are statistically few. However, of all the sentients, regardless of form, corporeal or otherwise, they come the closest to perceiving the true nature and essence of The All. Still not fully, though. Still limited. Still incomplete, unable to fathom or know The All in its complete fullness.

Now The All senses something awry within itself. Something off, out of balance.

THE FIFTH GUARDIAN: A SYMPHONY OF DISCORD

Disharmony. Broken Melodies. The All turns its attention to the Nexus.
The Voice awakens.

Bran Ty Jos – Despondent

Bran Ty Jos is drunk. Again. And broke. Again. The card game is going so well. The winning hand, his without question. Until the other gamer produces a stronger one. It does not make sense to Bran Ty. Nor does it help when he accuses the other of cheating. That earns him the loss of all his earnings, plus a rough escort out the back door into the alley behind the bar.

He still smarts from the bruises. Bruises earned after being picked up and tossed like a rag doll by the owner's burly helper. Well, at least being drunk has its advantages; the bruises could hurt a lot worse, but the strong drink lessens the pain. Then again, senses dulled, he cannot tell if anything is broken. The drink is a great balm to ease other pains too. His sister's death. His grief. His fault. His pain.

Perhaps this is a good time to seek out the consolation of a woman. At the very least, Jerine might take pity on him, and offer him something to ease the pain. Of course, there is Martara, but she loves him too much to put up with his nonsense. He does truly love her, but not enough to let go of his addictions, so she dismissed him. Jerine at least tolerates him. Maybe.

Last time they didn't part on the best of terms. Not when the creditors came looking for him, breaking down her door and he took off leaving her to deal with them. Risky to return, but worth a try. He straightens his tunic, confirms his trousers are still relatively clean and heads down the familiar path to her house, one he knows from memory, even in his intoxicated state.

He is almost there when he thinks his drunkenness has gotten the best of him. Jerine's dwelling is not to be seen. The whole area where her place should be is bathed in an extremely bright luminescence. Worse yet, it pulsates, driving its intensity right into his eyes, prematurely awakening the effects of the next day's hangover. Is that actually a doorway?

Overwhelmed, this citizen of the tenth planet from its star, in a relatively younger galaxy, part of the 121,984th universe, Bran Ty Jos, promptly throws up and passes out.

Martara continues to mourn. A Guardian glowers. A malfeasance chortles. A thread sleeps.

Interlude – Coalescence

It began coalescing an eternity ago. Negative destructive emotions and energies from countless universes and innumerable worlds across space and time, gathering from an unimaginable number of life forms, both lower biologicals and sentient beings. Anger. Fear. Rage. Hate. Loss. Grief. Jealousy. Despair. Pain. Purest Evil. So much more. So many more.

These wayward remnants of emotion wandered between the empty vastness of space for ageless millennia. Eventually, separately, they all found their way to the same destination. Over multiple spans of time, magnetically drawn together by their likeness, they slowly buried themselves deep within one of the earliest black holes on the outer fringes of the ever-expanding All.

It lies dormant for many lifetimes. Quiet. Still. Silent. Sleeping through immeasurable centuries, It did not mark or measure their passing. Biding Its time as It grew. Somewhere along the way It awoke, the beginning levels of a primitive consciousness taking shape.

It remained unmoving. Until It felt hunger.
Insatiable hunger.

Jason Toma – Chaos

Jason Toma's planet is nineteenth from its sun, part of a collection of twenty-five planets overall, within its universes' limited array of only five hundred galaxies. His planet has seen fit to evolve beings of immensely powerful gifts and abilities. By the Guardians' count, it is the 121,992 trillionth universe of The All.

Jason comes to, trying to sort out what just happened. Usually, he does his crime-fighting solo, but this time he decided it would be prudent to join forces with stronger allies. For the task at hand, this group's strengths complemented his heightened intelligence and ability to rapidly learn other combat styles. His fighting skills are bar none, yet it was his doing that led them into the ambush.

Uncertain how he missed something so obvious, he berates himself as he pulls the bullets from his armour. He holds one up to examine it. These are different, not the norm. His mind does a quick analysis. Power dampening bullets. He hears noises behind him. He turns and looks on in horror at his new allies lying on the ground, two already decapitated and a third about to be. He quietly climbs regains his footing while reaching into his belt. Silently withdrawing his slicers, he targets a sword-holder standing over the third fallen body. Jason's personal vow of only disable, never kill, succumbs to his anger and vanishes into the ether.

The slicer hits the assassin just above the nose, embedding itself deep into his forehead. Blood spurts out, coating the accomplice standing next to him. Jason's second slicer hits that one in the throat, catching the carotid artery, shutting off the blood supply to his brain. They are both done.

He catches up with the other two. His rage palpable, he speaks no words. They beg for mercy. Instead, he smashes their heads together and then rams both of their skulls repeatedly into the brick walls of the alley until blood flows from their ears, eyes and noses. One almost falls over, but he catches the man and snaps his neck. Jason believes he is being merciful. The other one, terrified, falls to the ground. Jason continues stomping on the man's head with his boot until his face caves in. He walks over to tend to what is left of his allies.

"Better to keep working alone," he mutters to himself.

Something laughs. A Guardian hesitates. Some mourn.
A thread frays.

Interlude – Nexus

The Nexus. Both by purpose and design, it is the way station. A gateway between all the worlds, universes, dimensions and myriad places of The All. The Nexus, more without The All than within it, yet both part of and not. The Nexus exists both within the flow of Space-Time and beyond it. For the Nexus, all Time is The Now. A holy tension, a tight thread, a taut tightrope holding The All within and outside of itself. Contradictory at the least, a conundrum beyond understanding at most.

Over an octillion years plus, with only a few exceptions of true genius or innocent, unassuming, childlike understanding, a relatively minuscule number of sentients were ever fortunate enough to find it. Those that did, consistently overwhelmed by it, grasped only its most rudimentary aspects.

For those sentients who do reach it while still in their corporeal forms, they see the Nexus in varying shapes. To some, it appears as a transportation depot. A hub for travel with different modes of transport to take one on a journey somewhere. The various modes of transportation they see are typically based on their culture. A true anthropological study.

Other sentients see a maze with different openings they might walk through, or fall through, if not careful. Some see a series of never-ending doors, mirrors or portals. Some sentients see wormholes or breaches, openings in space through a black backdrop of stars, filling the sky. Some view a quiet, peaceful forest with a series of innumerable pools that go on and on, as far as the eye can see. Abnormally calm pools that seem simultaneously inviting and dangerous.

Unfailingly, and without exception, the sentients who arrive ultimately choose a destination. They can not tolerate being nowhere indefinitely. Some reap what they sow. Others find great adventures. Some few make it back to try again. Something is different now though. The Nexus senses it. Feels it. Perceives it. Ponders it.

Bekka – Incurable

Bekka, leader of her tribe, currently camouflaged, stalks her prey. It will be more than a few million years before her race develops the term *apex predator*. She only knows that for the creature she currently hunts, she could just as easily be the prey, but will live longer if she acts as predator. She succeeds, killing the beast. A great victory, providing a good amount of food to take back to her people. She whistles, summoning the young men to come out of hiding so they may help carry the food back to the village.

Bekka is one of the elders in her tribe. Still with the vigour and energy of the young ones, mixed with the wisdom of experience, she is the ideal leader. Respected and well-liked. No one is about to challenge her for leadership, not yet. But that might come soon though. She does not understand what is happening to her, but something is not right. She is starting to forget things. Sometimes when out on a hunt she forgets where she is. That is dangerous, possibly deadly. She also has forgotten her way back to their village a few times. Over time, her memory grows worse; eventually she forgets most things.

She is exiled. Her people cannot risk her doing something foolish that will turn them into prey. She wanders aimlessly for a time. It's a miracle she survives as long as she does. Once, long ago when she was younger, some kind of black thing approached her. It touched her, then let her be. She has no recollection of that happening.

Here, on a world where forward development is painstakingly slow, part of a system with only three planets, within a rather humble galaxy, numbered 161,987[th] by the cosmic forces of creation, not yet very populated with stars or sentients, Bekka dies of starvation and dehydration. She has forgotten the importance of eating and drinking.

No one mourns. A Guardian thoughtful. A blackness pleased.
A thread forgotten.

Interlude – Instinct

At first, all Its actions are by instinct. It is driven by self-preservation alone.

It is also wary. Sly. Cautious. Predatory. It creates distractions and draws attention away from Its true purpose of feeding. While It seeks out prey, It simultaneously sends parts of Itself crawling across various places, testing Its strength. At times, It creates dark pockets to cover small fragments of creation and its life forms in blackness. It creates a void where existence once thrived.

The feeding needs to seem random. Easy enough, since parts of It had been in those places before. Not direct assaults: It starts with lower biological life forms. It mostly preys on them to absorb their fears. Then It discovers a higher form of biologicals. A form ripe with a massive variety of the emotions It relishes. It is still careful. It finds that influencing some of the higher biologicals, those most susceptible to Its dark will, comes easily. At times, It uses them to accomplish Its purposes. It makes it appear that Its victims are simply in the wrong place at the wrong time, a result of natural phenomena, such as nature, or the natural outcome of their actions. It must not allow any suspicions about the true malice behind the terminations. Misdirection comes to It naturally; It will not risk discovery. A dangerous predator, surviving by instinct alone. For now.

Instinct also tells It there is something else out there, but It knows not what. Perhaps a threat. Whatever the threat may be, It remains as hidden as It had been. It broods on this a while longer, then hunger and passion continue to drive It. The craving for sustenance is insatiable. The dark tendrils stretch out. They find a breach, a way in. Again. A small, almost indistinguishable hole in the fabric of space. A new universe full of worlds to seep into. Imperceptible. Random. Chaotic. Purposeless. The cessation of life threads easily attributed to the nature of the beings on this planet or in that galaxy. Subtly, craftily, so as not to bring attention to Its presence. Distraction and misdirection are excellent allies.

Still unnoticed by those who guard the balance,
It continues to satisfy Its hunger.

Tavez – Abandoned

It was a weird coming together of circumstances that gave their race the gift of flight. Even considering the infiniteness of The All, there are not that many species which have similarly developed. Perhaps a temporal anomaly or a bizarre blending of earlier ancestor and avian somewhere in the early origins of the gene pool. No one seems to know for sure in this 616,042,690th universe, as counted by The Guardians.

The ability to defy gravity and take flight without the aid of physical assistance is as common on this planet as is walking and breathing on so many others. It is not even that their kind have grown wings, it is just that sometime during adolescence, early on for some, later for others, but without exception, flying is a given. Eventually, everyone ends up being able to leap up and take to the skies. That is everyone without exception, until now.

Tavez is different. Not a late bloomer. Not disabled. Not mentally ill. Not sick.

He just, for no fathomable reason, cannot do it. It's not that he has not tried. Many times. Many bruises. Many rooftops, trees, whatever had height. His friends, well, former friends, just do it so naturally. A running leap and they are airborne. They don't need to start on some higher level to gain momentum and lift.

The doctors study him, test him. Psychologists, psychiatrists, specialists, run him through everything short of dissecting him, which sometimes Tavez fears they are going to do. They are intrigued by this strange mutation, and perhaps a bit frightened. What if he is the first of mutations that will eventually take over, their species then losing its capability of flight altogether? What if he is patient zero, carrying some kind of unidentifiable plague that will wreak havoc upon their world, killing off billions in the process?

There are even discussions with his parents, unbeknownst to him, of ensuring he is sterilized so he is unable to produce offspring and risk introducing his aberration into the general population. An interesting discussion, since his species evolved to be not genderless but rather multiple-genders capable. Meaning when one is fully sexually mature, they can call upon the necessary body parts to manifest as needed, depending on mood, desire, the company they keep and situation. Truly gender fluid, a rather unique attribute across the whole of The All.

This is not what is foremost on Tavez's mind though. He currently wanders through the streets, depressed, lost in thought, not paying attention to direction or location. His faithful four-legged furry companion, whom he's owned since early childhood, trots alongside him. Sensing his master's mood, the pet looks up at Tavez's face now and then to reassure him that he is not alone. It stops suddenly, voicing a growl indicating danger, causing Tavez to abruptly stop walking. When he becomes aware of where he is, it is too late. He recognizes the name on a vehicle and realizes it had likely been following him. It is from one of the less reputable research firms. He is not in one of the best areas of the city, not a place to easily call for help. He knows if he tries to leap into the sky, he will likely end up falling on his face, or worse, seriously injuring himself. Tavez chooses to run, his pet trailing him.

Unfortunately, he runs into two of the pursuers who left the van and circled around the block to prevent his escape. He turns to run the other way, but two more are waiting. His pet lunges for one of them, attempting to protect Tavez, but a gunshot puts the poor animal down without mercy. The four surround him. Devastated and furious over what they had just done, Tavez tries throwing a punch, misses and in return receives a nasty one in the face. A bag goes over his head. He is lifted and carried to the van. He tries to think about how he might escape. He knows this is bad.

He doesn't know how bad it is until they start to dissect him while he is still conscious. He screams from the horror and the pain until he finally passes out, praying he never wakes up again. He doesn't. The vivisection continues for many more hours.

His disappearance mourned. A terror delighted. A Guardian incensed. A thread disassembled.

THE FIFTH GUARDIAN: A SYMPHONY OF DISCORD

The barefoot little girl is going to meet someone.
She doesn't know who or where, but she knows they are important.
Very important.

Interlude - Harmony

Somewhere and some when, across and within the vastness of The All, exist Points of Origin for every original universe formed therein. Perhaps it started with just one original, followed by various iterations; perhaps there were more originals and then variations. Difficult to say now, amidst the countless number that exist, which ones might have been original, and which are all iterations from the original or are originals themselves.

Whatever the case, when the Cosmic Energies, Fundamental Forces and Powers of Creation collude together to bring new iterations into being, it is consistently because they decide someone, something, some world, galaxy or universe requires a course correction. Something is out of sync, lacking harmony, so a new version is created to administer healing and restore the original balance, original destiny or destinies, or whatever chords the Forces think should have been played. Harmony needs to be restored.

This fulcrum of Destiny gone astray, that forces the re-creation, is sometimes as simple as a sentient being's poor decision. Choosing a path that took their life off course and had an astounding butterfly effect on perhaps their whole world, if not galaxy, or in worst case scenarios, their entire universe. Other times, perhaps a natural or sentient-made catastrophe. A cataclysm of such proportions it was obviously never meant to be.

Sometimes an entire universe might decay or implode due to something in complete discord from the appointed path or original intent. Whose intent the Forces seem to understand, as they nudge with a minor chord or push with a major lift, ensuring whatever numbered iteration they recreate anew, does not meet the same fate. Harmonious again.

Naturally most life within The All remains blissfully unaware of this process.

CHAPTER TWO

Variations On a Theme – Staccato

In music, staccato is a playing technique where each individual note is sounded briskly. "Staccato" is Italian for "detached" or "disconnected."

Lindsay – Dawn

In this 661,986[th] universe, within its sixty-second galaxy, if one counts by the order that universes' galaxies came into existence, on a solar system close to this galaxy's northernmost outer limits, a tiny sphere, second from its sun, burgeoning with sentient humanoid life in the trillions, follows its appointed path around its star, oblivious of what is to come.

The mad dictator decides he has had enough. No more bullying. His nation-state will no longer tolerate the abuse, the sanctions, the so-called wisdom of those nations who claim they know better and offer a holier version of freedom to their peoples. They are infidels all and must burn. Something pushes him over the edge. Not that it matters what or who, in a post-apocalyptic world.

Lindsay Gallinger is asleep in her bedroom on the twenty-third floor of her fifty-nine-storey apartment building when the nuclear weapons begin bombarding the metropolis in which she lives. She wakes up as she plummets toward the ground, the noises around her a cacophony of sounds that drown out her screams. She manages to catch something as she drops, slowing her fall before she hits something solid. Her eyes are too covered in dust to see where she landed. Her last thoughts are, *"Is this it? Is this really all there is?"* Then unconsciousness.

Days later, a rescue team, garbed in protective suits, finds Lindsay covered in debris and radiation burns, but still breathing. They evacuate her to a makeshift hospital, set up to mostly watch people die anyway. The professionals debate if she will ever wake up from her coma, even if she survives the burns. They decide to wait a week before pulling the plug, assuming the generator lasts. They will all likely be dead soon enough anyway; the conflict has escalated to encapsule the whole world. The bombardments are unceasing. In her comatose state, Lindsay dreams of doing something significant. Something that will make the world a better place.

Few left alive to grieve. A darkness laughs. A Guardian hopes.
A thread dangles.

Interlude – Ravenous

It hungers. Deeply. Strongly. Wildly. It needs sustenance, something to satisfy a voracious appetite. Emotions. Not just any emotions though, It craves all those that will provide the dark energy needed to grow stronger. Impenetrable even. A force of nature that will not be quelled.

It slowly begins to seek out additional pathways to find more of the energy essential for survival and an increase in power. Biological beings, life forms of all kinds. Consistently, bundles of grief, rage, anger, despair, desolation, fury and fear, are everywhere It seeks. How delicious. How satisfying. How delectable. How delightful. It must be careful though. Not ready to reveal Itself yet, not fully. These are trial runs.

A nudge here, a push there, as It continues to grow stronger. It finds new ways to prey upon the biologicals. Not overtly, It will not dare that, not yet. It stays an unseen puppet master, pulling others' strings from behind the curtain. It tests Its own limits, from affecting births to the infliction of deadly diseases, even plagues. Quietly, infecting a biological with a contagion or virus from another universe, easily implanted without notice. The resulting loss, grief and agony provides more nourishment.

It also finds ways to influence the higher-level biologicals that have similar leanings to Its own abundance of grim feelings. It tempts these sentient beings to take their emotions one step further, to do the next deplorable, unspeakable thing. They are completely unaware of the presence of the dark tendril enticing them, thinking it was all them. The Dark Thing knows better. How easy it is to manipulate these pitiful creatures. Carefully, though. Still unseen. Still secretive. Always ravenous. It no longer feeds just out of need, but also for pleasure.

It enjoys perceiving the colours of the beings' life threads dissolve as their lives slip away. It is not only growing, but It is learning. The basics of a rudimentary intelligence begin to form. Though It might not have been as discreet as It thought.

The All and The Nexus converse. The Guardians stand ready.
The Darkness unaware.

Ty Bran – Disheartened

On a close, but not precise replica of what its inhabitants in another universe call Earth, with more similarities than differences, it is exactly one year after the funeral. Also, it is Ty Bran's twenty-first birthday. How pathetically ironic. Exactly how he thinks of himself since his sister's accident: pathetic. Well, *his* accident; she was collateral damage. God, that sounds so cold. The guilt still overwhelms him, he cannot shake it.

Now Ty lies semi-conscious in the middle of the road. His best friend Garr stands off to the side, laughing uncontrollably at his friend's intoxicant-fueled immobility. Garr sincerely believes he is giving his friend the greatest twenty-first birthday celebration ever by getting him thoroughly drunk.

Garr is positive this will help Ty move past his guilt and have fun again. Finally, be himself again, living it up and moving on with his life. Besides, there is nothing more hilarious than watching his friend give in to the effects of the high levels of alcohol in his system and languish in a frozen stupor, in such an awkward place and position. Garr watches as the joke reaches its climax.

Ty barely feels the weight of the vehicle as it crushes his body, bones broken as more than two tons of metal rolls over his covering of flesh. A sharp part of the undercarriage tears his throat open, removing his ability to breathe. For a moment, in that undefinable period between life and death, even in his blurred state, Ty glimpses something beyond his normal range of vision, something indistinguishable, yet far greater than himself. A surprising revelation that he has missed something significant. More regret. On this tiny, ninth planet within the twelfth galaxy close to another, called by some sentients, Andromeda, Ty Bran's universe quivers.

THE FIFTH GUARDIAN: A SYMPHONY OF DISCORD

Many mourn. A Guardian saddened. A shadow cheers.
A thread motionless.

Interlude – Iterations

The other interesting aspect to The All's universal recreation process is that the farther out the iterations move away from the original, the more varied things become, including the beings who populate The All. A new iteration close to the point of origin often spawns very similar worlds, people, places, if not almost identical to the original, with only very slight, almost unnoticeable differences. However, the farther out the iterations move away from the original, the more pronounced changes become, even to the point where some sentients might not even be on the same planet in their solar system, and differences could include such facets as gender, race, species, even epoch.

Naturally, corrections continue even with the new iterations which might have been considered the originals, depending on one's point of view. Two things, however, always remain consistent for sentient life forms across all the re-creations, no matter how far out they may be from the original. One is the framework for an appellation; whatever the original being's name might be, there is always some variant of it in their replicas across The All. Whether a slight change, such as becoming a middle or last name, or portion thereof, there remains some recognizable structure to the individual sentient's designation. Harmony continues or is at least close, while further iterations less and less so.

Secondly, as far as sentient beings are concerned, there is unfailingly at least one common theme that follows them and is part of their existence, regardless of which variation of a universe in which they exist. Sometimes so different from the original, their variation could be anywhere from a prehistoric age, an advanced civilization, a post-apocalyptic era or a faster-than-light-travel society. The same melody persists throughout The All in every version of every universe, in the life of every variation. Without fail, the same theme or themes continue to play out in their lives. These two consistent facets, nomenclature and theme, will serve the Guardians well in their mission.

Unfortunately, they will also aid something ill-intentioned in Its search too.

Jason (J.T.) – Covenant

In a galaxy bordering very close to its nearest neighbour, within a universe designated as 1992, the nineteenth day of the month on this twelfth planet from its sun begins like most others for J.T. as he briefs his small squad. They joke again about what to call themselves and eat a quick breakfast together. They are supranormals, all three of them, four if you count Jason, called J.T., their leader. Speed, Flight, Magic, Elemental; a good combo. Any names they come up with sound ridiculous, so they refer to themselves only as The Squad.

Time for duty, the usual boring stuff, nothing out of the ordinary. Checking into this complaint, that dispute, maybe a robbery or two, a vehicle theft, a school bullying situation, nothing major. All investigated and closed by lunch time. This has become mundane and boring. Until it isn't.

The communications system at the station lights up: multiple homicides, three school shootings and terrorists in at least four different major locations in the city. Is this a joke? All at once? The squad takes off, splitting up. It's the best way to put these fools down. Two will help with the closest incidents quickly, provide back up to the investigating officers and regroup with J.T. and their comrade at the first reported terrorist location.

J.T. is the first on one of the terrorist scenes, flying in, dressed in full body armour. Also, the first to take the hit from an armour-piercing shell that splits his protective gear open. The next one rips into his chest. An ambush! Where is his squad? He tries flying up, but something holds him down. Magic! A blur runs circles around him, sucking the air out of his already damaged lungs. No idea why his squad is betraying him. An external force? Is something or someone else controlling them? Or have they just chosen to go rogue? No time to decide. Payback is a bitch. He manages to free one hand enough to activate the emergency kill switch, frying their brains and turning their bodies into ash. His closest friends; he just crossed a line, broke a promise. The lives of good people taken. Maybe not so good. Is it better to press his own kill switch and end it?

A wickedness cackles. A Guardian despairs. All mourn. A thread splits.

Interlude – Relentless

As Its intelligence grows, It settles on a more deliberate strategy: one not just based on instinctive reactions. Now a strategy that is thoughtful, focused, organized, intentional. Carefully constructed to avoid detection and work towards solid goals. A strategy, smart, achievable, realistic and timed to the nanosecond to ensure actions remain hidden and undetectable, without drawing cause for alarm. Cautious, but determined and well-orchestrated. The notes of discord that might be caused by Its actions buried amidst distraction and deceit. A duplicitousness that could be well-used to Its advantage by speeding up the process to eliminate all threats detected. Not only is this a new method of hunting prey, but it is also exciting, invigorating, enticing, thrilling, satisfying. The anticipation enticing.

As Its sojourns of gluttony continue, over time the Thing begins to recognize something: Its gradually forming intelligence and long memory register that occasionally It comes across beings elsewhere in the vastness like ones already dispatched. Even the colours of their life threads are a match, regardless of what universe in which It found them.

This is both interesting and confusing to the creature's growing intellect. Even disturbing. How is it possible that at times, almost identical beings are dispersed throughout Its feeding grounds? It decides to make a game of it, eliminating as many of the similar ones as possible. It only needs to discover their identical life threads by spreading Its tendrils out across the infinite spaces to detect them, and then end them by whatever discreet means chosen. Although It does not know the word, It is having fun. Addictive, relentless, fun.

A Darkness hunts. Guardians suspect. Biologicals mourn.
Threads at risk.

Rebecca - Terminal

The paddles ripple the water gently as the canoe glides forward on the calm river. Sounds of the woods; birds, insects, animals in the forest that bank either side the only disturbance, which adds to the calmness. The two figures are quiet, lost in thought, silence between them.

They have come for one last time. She needs to enjoy the peacefulness. They need the time together, just them. Becca's full name is Rebecca, which she was never fond of, so she had shortened it to Becca by kindergarten. Short and to the point, just like her. What an odd thought to have out here.

She looks at her husband. His brow furrows, he cannot relax, he loves her so much. She knows if she starts speaking, they will both cry again. She thinks of their children; she will miss them. Lord, they are still reeling from the deaths of both sets of grandparents. A combination of old age and freak, tragic accidents. Her husband wonders how he can go it alone without her. Raise the children, do everything. He will, but thinking about it makes it worse.

The cancer is spreading. After the last exam, they discovered it now fills her entire body. They gave her days yet she has lasted almost two weeks. Too stubborn to give in before she says all her goodbyes. She reaches out to hold his hand. Something stops her. She feels something odd touch her and pulls her hand back for a moment. Perhaps it is pain from the cancer, but not like she has felt before. Then it is gone.

The dark visitor sees that nature has already done its work. It departs. No need for intervention on this sixteenth planet in a rapidly aging universe, one of the highest numbered ones amidst The All.

Becca reaches out again and clasps her husband's hand. They both cry, sob, then go home. The palliative team give her just enough drugs to ease the pain but still allow her to remain conscious. The next morning, surrounded by her loving family and a few close friends, she slips away to meet her Lord.

Her family mourns. A Guardian uncertain. An Ill-Will ponders.
A thread exits.

Interlude – Destiny

The Guardians are becoming aware now. There are vague signs that a malevolent Darkness has slipped in, ever so subtly. Invisible, unseen, blending in, hidden in plain sight. A rustling of the leaves, like a soft, quiet, gentle breeze barely moving them. The results are hardly noticeable but they are unmistakably there. Enough to indicate something is amiss, an infinitesimal, almost undetectable discord in the musical harmony that is the symphony of The All.

In odd places, the Guardians observe destinies chosen out of sync with what other factors dictated should have been. In a few isolated lonely instances, pasts and futures merge in ways that indicate lines crossed, that should not have normally been so. Definite signs of something gone awry. Anomalies that defy explanation, except for the one that does yield an answer. An explanation unwanted and unwelcome, but now its acceptance inevitable.

At first the Guardians wondered if Chaos was the culprit, but their cosmic level of perception negated that. Chaos, always part of the natural process, was not the enemy here. The Guardians understood there was always Order in Chaos; as it found its way through all creations, it replaced Order with something newer. Hurricanes could leave a new beach in their aftermath, simply part of the natural way of things within The All. The Guardians did not seek to prevent this, rather allowed it to follow its course, even if at times it meant death and destruction for universes, galaxies or the many varied life-forms inhabiting them. It is natural. This is not.

This time, lofty cosmic senses are unable to discern the source. Hidden, pernicious, almost imperceptible, beneath the cover of Chaos. Using Chaos as a cloak, a deceptive nothingness. Camouflaged, wisely, smartly, buried deeply behind, letting Itself be quietly carried on the winds of Chaos, with Chaos being an unknowing ally. The will behind this, determined to destroy destinies, so far unknown and unknowable.

The Guardians concerned. The Nexus disturbed. The foe hidden. Threads of destiny in danger.

TV – Solo

Perhaps it is due to the myriad of cosmic forces at work, or the playfulness of the quantum energies involved, or something more sinister or less indulgent during the replication process as a new universe forms, along with its galaxies, planetary systems, astronomical phenomena and the eventual creation of sentient life.

Whatever the case, a planet is spawned in a system that as most, quietly orbits its star in a regular rotation measured in years, which becomes home to a species of sentient life that for whom multiple births is the norm. Multiple births in terms of twins, triplets, or as they called them, triads, or in more than a few scenarios, quads, or quadruplets and sometimes, though not as frequently, quintuplets, or quints.

The population is obviously very fertile. In fact, this occurs not just in the sentient beings' births, but in the planet's animal kingdom, as well as in aquatic and avian species. It is the norm for pretty much all living things on this world. What is not the norm, and this only happens with the sentients, rather than with the other species on the planet, is single births. Solos, as they are called, are random and rare.

Worse, they are an embarrassment to their families, as they inevitably develop some type of birth defect, visible or invisible. It often grows worse as they age and the more severe cases mean that those particular "Solos" will not live past their coming of age during puberty. Often this is both a moment of grief and relief for family, friends and the individual themselves. They will no longer have to carry the stigma of being a burden and an embarrassment to those around them, even those that loved them. For many Solos, the end is a very welcome place.

Not for TV though, pronounced *Tee-Vee* with a strong emphasis on the longer drawn out *Vee* portion, something he decided upon during early childhood. Unfortunately, it is also something that makes him stand out, along with an already challenging speech impediment, one that often causes him to stutter or slur his words.

He was the source of many jokes, from both family members, the few people he could call genuine friends and schoolmates, who were often hardly mates. School was composed of relentless bullies in his life, determined to never let him forget how different, how much lesser he was than the twins, triads, quads and quints he was surrounded by.

Whether it was because of his natural easy-going nature, his positive attitude, his overall charm or his recognition that there were others like him with far worse impediments, from fatal diseases to being born with grotesque disfigurements, he stayed true to his heart. He was ever a faithful friend, respectful, always ready to lend a helping hand to others regardless of their class in society. He just didn't know any better or know any different; that is how he lived and grew. He grew past and out of the puberty stage that was the expected death-knell for so many of his Solo peers. His family and friends were impressed, others not so much. Perhaps it was his kind, gentle nature that was his undoing.

TV had just reached out to help a younger first year Solo currently being beaten badly by the regular cadre of school bullies. So pronounced is the racism and prejudice on this planet that such behaviour is not only condoned, but also encouraged. People this radically different really do not deserve to live; they were likely going to die anyway, so there is no harm in speeding up the process. This is the belief of the one who prevents TV from helping up their beaten victim by whacking him across the back of the head with what in some civilizations would be called a baseball bat. A second uses their sports equipment as well; an instrument shaped like a javelin pierces TV's leg. He starts stuttering, begging for them to stop.

This only infuriates them more, so another two from the group start to repeatedly kick and punch him. For good measure, the others do the same to the younger boy who TV had tried to help.

EMS takes their sweet time to arrive. When they do, without compassion, but rather with relief, they bag the bodies and drop them off at the mortuary for cremation. No investigation or autopsy is ever required for these situations; too much paperwork. No point wasting time on people who are lesser.

A family mourning, yet relieved. A hidden thing glad.
A Guardian livid. A thread shrivels.

Interlude – Strategy

Occasionally through the hunting game, a specific impression draws the creature's interest: destiny. It is not yet able to grasp the full meaning of the word but understands that Its feeding is somehow affecting the destiny of these biologicals. Changing a path, or bringing the biologicals' destiny to an unexpected end, It adds the idea to Its repertoire. Affecting destinies becomes as much of an amusement as eliminating the identical biologicals themselves.

It relishes the damage and destruction of all living things, taking great delight as the different colours of their life threads dissipate. Naturally, this does not stop the random feeding on others not identical. It is still ravenous after all and the basic instinctive strategy remains. It continues to maintain the appearance of randomness until a unique encounter occurs.

During one of Its feeding frenzies, as a biological life form meets its gruesome end, the being's life thread both glows and vibrates in way not detected before. Its every sense within screams, *DANGER!* Its entire being shakes and roars *BEWARE!* This is new. Unprecedented. It has already learned to track and extinguish multiples of biologicals across different universes. Yet this difference is dangerous to Its own existence. It does not understand how or why, but knows it to be true.

This truth inspires a new mission, a mission of self-preservation. No more random feeding; It has an objective. Save Itself from whatever threats to Its existence are out there. It must track and destroy all the biologicals who possess the uniquely-coloured life threads that vibrate in the same way as the one just ended, no matter where they might be found. It is essential to Its own survival that they be destroyed, their life threads dissolved, their destinies ended or at the very least damaged so significantly that they are no longer a threat. It prefers the former over the latter, but will settle for either, as long the threat ceases to be.

It has a mission. An objective. A strategy. Dark strands reach out.
Searching.

The barefoot little girl with wavy blond hair meets a talking animal on her walk. It reminds her of a unicorn. Although not one like any from the picture books she remembers. She and the sort-of-unicorn engage in a wonderfully interesting conversation about the importance of having toast on one's birthday. When it is over, she continues walking.

She is on her way to meet Someone. Someone very important.

CHAPTER THREE

Variations on a Theme – Allegro

Allegro is a tempo marking indicating to play fast, quickly and bright.

Interlude - Expelled

Two Guardians turn their minds to focus on the end of a thread, a path to where a sentient just experienced a painfully gruesome end to their existence. They are too late to intervene, the deed done before they become aware, one of the drawbacks of not being omniscient.

Nevertheless, this is fortuitous; it means whatever dark thing they seek has both arrived and left. Two trails to follow, one to backtrack and one with which to track forward. They consult internally and one chooses the former whilst the other Guardian opts for the latter. The path forward seemingly ends shortly before it started; something is not right. The Guardian senses it but is unable to discern why the trail so abruptly ceases. The Guardian hesitates, deciding to purposely pause, allowing for more focus on the point at which the trail terminated. Whatever was there has vanished, leaving no trace. How odd. The Guardian tries once more to discern deeper. It feels a twinge from something powerful, dark, angry, malevolent and determined. The Guardian senses a push against its own formidable being and then it is gone. Somehow, it has evaded even the Guardian's keen cosmic perception.

The other Guardian follows the trail backwards. It is straightforward at first, the sense of some entity, easily followed. Then it begins to take twists and turns, looping back in upon itself, then around in circles, traversing Space-Time in strange unpredictable ways.

Obviously, it does not wish to be found. Perhaps this is no mere animalistic creature, acting only on primal urges. This is purposeful and cunning, perhaps strategic with intent. Whatever the Guardian attempts to follow does not wish to be found. The Guardian persists and reaches a point in the path on the edge of discovery. Unexpectedly, something ragged and sharp tears at the edges of the Guardian's conscience. The Guardian pushes back, but whatever force this thing possesses is formidable. The Guardian glimpses the shape of a dark, nebulous hole before it tumbles away, spinning out of control. This has never happened before in any of the Guardian's recollections. Unthinkable!

A Guardian expelled. A darkness alerted. Potents endangered.
Threads at risk.

Lindsay – Sunrise

Sixty-six universes away, forty-two galaxies in, on the ninth planet orbiting its double star, in a solar system near the galaxies' mid-point, Lindsay Bellinger ponders the future. Early morning, the sun just rising and the beach is already attracting a decent crowd. People are trying to find the best spots before the crowd grows too large on what promised to be a sweltering, clear day.

She stands on the shore after her early run along the beach, her feet cooling in the soothing, small waves that make their way inland. She enjoys the feeling of the sand shifting between her toes. Her Master's in Science now complete, graduating with Highest Honours, she carries on an internal conversation about what was next. PhD? Medical School? A walkabout for a year to take a break? Maybe overseas? Then there is that boy. Doing something significant. Making a difference. Just as her parents taught her and modelled for her. Yes, definitely.

The shooter appears as randomly as the bullets he fires. Lindsay hears odd popping noises, turns and sees a child fall. Her mother screams and drops too. Instinctively, she runs to help. Bad idea. A bullet rams into her leg, causing her to fall in the sand, the pain searing. She tries to stand, also a bad idea. Another bullet crashes into her chest, embedding itself into her heart. She falls again, the pain worse.

Through her tears, she sees panicking people running in every direction, seeking refuge, some into the water, others towards their cars in the parking lot. Many fall; nowhere is safe. Her parents are coming to see her at the cottage tonight. How awful. She feels blood fill her lungs. As life ebbs from her body, her last thoughts float uselessly, *"Nothing significant now. How ridiculously unfair."* And she is gone.

THE FIFTH GUARDIAN: A SYMPHONY OF DISCORD

Her parents grieve. A malice smiles. A Guardian mourns.
A thread ceases.

Interlude – Discovery

It does not like what It felt. The pain reverberates throughout Its entire form, carried by the tendrils that had encountered the force which discovered and challenged It. It does not recognize these creatures. They are nothing like the biologicals but they are formidable, unlike Its' usual, easily manipulated prey. They tracked It despite Its skills at staying unseen. They found It, or at least some of Its extensions sent out to do Its work. They began to backtrack to Its centre. It took all Its strength and a massive amount of willpower to push the almost indomitable force back before drawing too close. It succeeded, but at great cost, Its energy is depleted. It needs to feed. A lot. Yet not take another risk of discovery. Instinctively It pauses and rests. Its hunger growing along with something else: rage.

Something besides rage as well. As It pauses, brooding over the encounter, flashes of insight begin to form, impressions left by the unknown foe. Knowledge from Its oppressor somehow transferred over to Its own thoughts. Foreign pictures form in Its developing mind. A new word takes shape: Nexus.

The word echoes throughout Its being, Nexus. A glimmer of comprehension begins. Nexus. Both a threat and a solution. A gateway. A gathering place of pathways, to every part of creation within The All. So that is what the entirety of this is: The All. How delicious! If It could find this Nexus, It would have access to everything.

It could extend Itself through every opening, expand and gather everything into Itself, submerging it in Its own Darkness. Or even better, perhaps It could simply envelop the Nexus entirely. Then, at Its leisure, slowly consume everything, until all the portals and pathways to every single part of The All are within Itself. Relishing the taste of every collapsed element of creation as It gradually devours it, piece by delectable piece, ultimately leaving everything completely devoid of life, including The All.

The Darkness seeks a new goal. An unknown enemy seeks It.
A growing awareness in both. A race.

Bran Jos – Desperate

On the sixth planet in orbit around its star, a young Bran Jos sucks in a fresh breath of methane from the crisp morning air prior to donning the helmet that will complete his flame-heat resistant suit. Within a galaxy that is part of a very young universe, 12,001,984th within The All to be exact, Bran Jos's methane-breathing people live on a planetary body known as a gas giant, actually the tenth planet in their solar system.

Bran Jos's people are not advanced enough yet to know this fact. They know their home only as Neerwitmar. They have not even begun to consider flight of any kind as a possibility. However, they are learning to be masters of the flaming seas. These seas make up the highest percentage of the planet. Large land masses are much less in abundance, as the planet consists of innumerable islands spread across the globe.

Waterway travel, just beginning, thanks to the discovery of a heat-resistant resin, allows people from islands close by to meet and learn from each other. This is not about conquest or territorial expansion; that is not in the nature of the peoples of Neerwitmar. They still do not venture too far beyond the closest islands and peoples they discover. Their vessels are not quite ready for longer voyages.

They are always prepared for friendly competitions with the peoples of the nearest islands though and this morning's race is just that. It is what Bran Jos has been preparing for. Ever since the accident, he has sought something that would give him focus. For a long time he blamed himself, carrying the overwhelming guilt as an unrelenting burden, until he knew better.

Through the support of family, friends and his refreshed faith in The Powers, he finally found peace and focus. The competitions are part of that, not all, not everything, but he is good. A good racer. His scuttle, self-made, is one of the shining stars in the races, pride of his people, and an instrument of focus and satisfaction for Bran Jos. Named for his sister, a peace offering, an ode to an unbearable tragedy, it helps to bring him closure.

Bran was so young when it happened. In some civilizations he would be considered an old man, by the way they count time. Due to the planet's slow sojourn around its sun and the way his species evolved, at seventy cycles, or as some might count them, seventy years, Bran is just now leaving adolescence. No wonder he struggled with his sister's fate; he was still very much a child himself back then.

There are times when he wonders what might have become of him if he had taken a different path in his grief. If he had not listened, not sought help, had lost his faith completely, what might his life have become? These days he does not dwell too long on these thoughts when they surface, but he understands his life would be very different from the one he lives now.

Bran stands on the scuttle, fully outfitted in his protective gear, his mind on the race. The tri-horn sounds. The scuttles begin their run from Bran Jos's island to the next closest. The racers find their speeds, interchanging places, gaining and falling behind, over and over in an almost musical rhythm. The morning is perfect, the air clear, the sun bright; for a change, the sky lacks the usual cloudy spots emitted randomly by the gas giant's superstructure.

He glances up to see the sky slowly begin to grow darker. Something crawls at the fringes of the planet's sun, edging its way across the glowing orb. So odd. Bran's people don't yet know the term eclipse, nor is it one. Bran stares at the sky, losing focus. Too late, another scuttle, its pilot also staring up, loses control and crashes hard into Bran's ship, sending Bran overboard.

Bran watches the seeping darkness overshadow the light and feels time drag. He falls in slow motion, a jagged jerking of his body on the way down, a bit at a time, until he finally drops into the flaming sea, submerged in its depths.

The flame-heat-resistant gear is designed only for enough time to survive a brief exposure to the planet's fiery seas, before one is quickly pulled up. Bran's face mask fogs over. The sea's boiling heat clashes against his suit. He doesn't have long. He sinks, helplessly lost in time and sea, waiting for the inevitable end.

An island mourns. A Guardian perplexed. A darkness advances.

A thread submerges.

Interlude – Unnamed

The Guardians regroup and discuss their discovery. The Guardian is uncertain if the creature has been damaged in the battle of wills. It is unclear if It had skulked away or left in victory. Whatever the case, something dark and powerful has taken shape. Something likely hidden for eons. Dangerous. Something Unnamed. Something powerful enough to threaten the existence of The All. If It found its way to the Nexus, all of creation, every universe, every life within each, could be blotted out. It must be stopped. It has tried to hide Itself again. The Guardian caught a brief glimpse though. Perhaps enough to determine a location.

The Guardians reach out collectively to the Nexus, projecting the image of a dark, nebulous hole. Requesting aid in identifying where in The All this Unnamed threat is to be found. The Nexus, oddly enough, remains silent, its attention is elsewhere. The Guardians try again, still no response.

The Guardians patiently wait. Finally, something. A hesitation. A caution. A warning projected back. The Guardians understand. If they could see the Unnamed thing, It might see them. Could see the Nexus. Could have every pathway to every place in The All open to It. Not a good option. The Guardians acknowledge that a different tactic must be employed.

The Guardians wait. The Unnamed waits. The All contemplates. The Nexus considers.

Jason T. – Contract

In a galaxy bordering very close to its nearest neighbour, within a universe designated as 1,991,219, the night on this fifth planet from its sun begins like most others for Jason T. Dressed in protective camouflage, he begins on the rooftops, scouring the streets below for any signs of trouble or people he can help.

He is a conflicted individual. Violent in the extreme, yet vowing never to take a life, a line he refuses to cross, a contract with himself. He comes close sometimes. Evil is just that, but he refuses to become as bad as those who perpetrate it. He carries no traditional weapons but enough other items to do the job.

Law enforcement doesn't always know what to do with him. Vigilantes shouldn't be allowed to run loose doing what they want. On the other hand, they appreciate his assistance, particularly with some of the more difficult, more dangerous elements. Known by many nicknames, he prefers Justice. At least that is what he hopes he is doling out. Even if it takes a few solid punches to the face or gut to get the message across. A broken arm or leg might do the job just as well sometimes, too.

A scream. What is that down below in the alley? Slain children? *"My god, what are they doing to the bodies?"* More screams, the parents? *"More kids getting sliced up?"* He leaps down into the midst of the fray, anger welling up. He takes out the killers in no time. Fury and wrath consume him. He breaks their necks. Justice! They have no chance. Neither did he. A sniper's bullet grazes his face. He has been too caught up in his rage to pay attention to his surroundings. A second rips into the lower part of his face, where the protective mask doesn't cover. He bends over but does not fall. Pain now. Ire. Rage. Hate.

The snipers are on the ground now, drawing closer, one per side. Jason

T. picks up two of the knives, children's blood still dripping from them. The snipers are overconfident. They don't see his motion and drop to the ground when the knives penetrate their jugulars, killing them instantly. What has he done? Crossed the line, broken his vow, defiled his contract. He will live, but he knows he cannot do this any more.

A wickedness celebrates. A Guardian disheartened. A city mourns.
A thread unravels.

Interlude – One-offs

Every now and then, it seems the forces of Creation, the Quantum Powers and whatever else is involved in the conspiracy, take a holiday by doing something rather unique. As though they have forgotten their original purpose of restoring balance through replication, they do something unpredictable. Either as part of a new iteration of a universe or sometimes just something created absent-mindedly, dimensions spring into being.

At least that is the term, or some form of its meaning, used by most sentients. Dimension, meaning something set apart, not a normal part of the whole, different from the regular world. Some of these dimensions birth into existence attached to a new version of a universe but live just outside of its normal flow of Space-Time. In some cases, it is connected through a pathway to the universe it is attached to, and other times not connected at all. It is just there, outside the normal boundaries of its universe, existing unaware to its many sentient neighbours.

Other dimensions exist in the space or gap between universes, not attached to anything. These are the interesting ones that might offer multiple pathways to various locations across The All. More remarkable are two constants: both the creatures that populate these various dimensions and secondly, the normal laws of physics so common across the universes of The All, rarely apply within these one-offs.

Gravity, Space, even Time, are a melting pot of bizarre randomness, such that any sentients who might ever dare to cross over into these places are totally confused by what they see and how things function. It is abnormal to most, the stuff of nightmares to many. Perhaps there is order to dimensional random chaos, but if so, it is difficult to find. Dimensions are typically discordant and outside the norm. If they ever left to enter a different universe or world, they would undoubtedly experience the same confusion and chaos in reverse.

The Guardians ignore the dimensions.
Dark tendrils discover multiple entranceways across The All.

Beckett – Toxic

Beckett cannot recall their beginnings in the dimension they call home, sometimes they have flashes of being somewhere else. Visions of a totally different type of environment and falling through some type of fissure or crack in the ground while others helplessly watch. There is another memory though, of just kind of popping into existence as one of the energy beings that populate this oddly-shaped reality. A reality that morphs, mutates and resets itself on numerous occasions.

There are other beings living in the dimension as well, besides the ones with disembodied, untethered consciousnesses like Beckett. Things that are more biological than energy-based, or sometimes a hybrid of both, but that is currently the problem. Stated more correctly, Beckett is the problem, and those two latter forms of beings are after them, en masse.

They are hunting them for something Beckett is not even sure they are responsible for, but it is possible. Maybe it is related to their poorly-recalled origins. Beckett is what the creatures who chase them refer to as, *"The Zero."* It means they believe Beckett is the initial carrier of the plague that started to infiltrate their domain a few cycles ago.

Even as an energy form, Beckett feels something not right within their being, but cannot identify what it is. By the time Beckett determines that they are the source, it is too late. Two thirds of the inhabitants have been wiped out, succumbing to the contagion; a virulent disease, causing violent pain and agony until, whether organic or hybrid, their forms dissipated into nothingness in colourful explosions. The irony is not lost on Beckett.

The lack of the normal physical laws that exist in most universes within The All, make the hunt for Beckett much more difficult. Beckett is unaware of these differences, knowing only this dimension as their home.

Here gravity does not obey natural laws of other universes and neither does matter, energy or other aspects of physics. Beckett can jump from place to new place with a thought or dematerialize into solid matter and reappear again. Beckett learned from a young age how to create real-life solid constructs from pictures in their mind and they now use this skill to hide and protect themselves from their pursuers.

They are doing so well too, that is until their own pain suddenly catches them unaware. They find themselves dematerializing from energy into a form of matter which makes the intensity of the pain worse. This happens multiple times, as their constructs lose their solidity and vanish, leaving Beckett visible and vulnerable to those who hunt them. Beckett senses the hunters are drawing nearer. As the pain grows, they realize something else as well, something horrible. Something disastrous. Something life and world ending.

Beckett couldn't know that the disease was an unwelcome gift left inside them by a black tendril that had trailed them following the hue of their thread. How convenient though, as it left its mark and then passed through, using the dimension as a gateway to other destinations.

The pursuers arrive. They bend their forces toward Beckett. Mind energies and matter attack. Beckett in all sincerity tries to warn them off. Too late. They are too incensed to hear, too angry, too furious to understand. Their fear and grief consume them and drive them into a frenzy. All they want, all they desire, is to end Beckett.

They do, and in so doing, they end themselves. Unlike the others who have already perished, Beckett's death blast is totally dark. The resulting explosion of deep blackness spreads like a plague across the entire dimension, engulfing everything in a wave of annihilation, death and destruction. It does not just wipe out all life in the dimension, it wipes out the existence of the dimension itself.

In the seconds before it too is obliterated, a piece of the dark tendril still inside Beckett uses its telepathic connection to send waves of the exponentially growing anger, fear and terror of the sentients back to its Master, as their dimension and all within it, self-destruct. The Master rejoices and wallows in gluttonous satisfaction.

A mirror darkens. A Guardian shocked. An evil grins.
A thread explodes.

Interlude - The Voice

The Guardians recognize it immediately. Whether audible or only an echo in their combined consciousness is impossible to discern, they know it though. Even though they cannot remember the last time it spoke, it is easily familiar. Overwhelming. Thunderous. Loud as a whisper and quiet as a solar storm. Perhaps the last time was only at the very origin of the Guardians themselves. They have no recollection of other times, though memories that ancient may be excused if they are forgotten. No matter, the message is clear. The Voice speaks to the Guardians, imprinting upon them a new mission or at least, a modified mission. Their role is still to guard The All but now they are given a new way of doing so.

The Guardians wonder about The Voice. Wonder if it is the Nexus speaking to them, if perhaps, it is more than just a gateway. They wonder if it is The All somehow embodying itself into a single Voice that reaches out to them, calling them to aid in its survival. Or is it from outside The All? Something Else entirely? Source indeterminate. No matter. The primary Mission given in the beginning, still holds: Guard The All. Now though, there is a new direction in how to fulfill that Mission.

The Voice speaks again, flooding them with images. Visions of multiple universes, countless worlds, sentients, destinies. The message is clear, the order is distinct. The task is daunting, though doable. The Voice shows them. The Voice tells them. The Voice conscripts and commands.

Protect The All. Follow the threads. Seek the Potents. Unique hues. Distinct vibrations. The Voice goes silent. The Guardians wait no longer.

Varez – Isolated

Varez's slim, black hands move deftly upon the Tab controlling the Explorer out at the far edge of his galaxy. It is the only part of him that does work. A genetic mutation, manifested during early childhood, left the rest of him immobile, confined to a bed. Eventually, with the help of a specialized mechanical chair, he gained some limited mobility. It was a blessing in disguise. He became smart. Super genius level. Unlike anyone before him.

Even so, to this day there are still the naysayers. The race wars ended long ago but that doesn't mean generational bigotry and prejudice were completely erased from Varez's civilization. The original blue- and green-skinned colonizers finally relented and ended centuries of slavery, freeing people from the generational poverty that had kept Varez's ancestors subjugated, or worse.

Freedom came at a great cost for many, and though it arrived at least two centuries before Varez was born, some still viewed his people as so different, so "other," that they were worthless and undeserving. Those sentiments linger in hidden corners, waiting for the opportunity to resurface into the light and reclaim their rightful place of control and domination of the hated and despised Other.

Varez may still be seen as an aberration by those hate-mongers but even they have to admit that his theories and their practical applications have revolutionized technology on their world. Computers, climate control, food supply, the elimination of poverty, advances in physics, chemistry, communication and transportation, right up to space travel. The first manned flights to their two satellite moons, have happened within the last year. Faster-than-light travel is next. It has already been done with computerized robots. The world government idolizes him, the people love him. Even the Tab he currently uses, a mini-brain, is mostly his invention.

His world's long-range telescope revealed something moving out near the edge of the galaxy. The astronomers were intrigued. They asked the government for assistance. Varez was immediately contacted and given the mission. At first, he wonders if this is some new formation of a black hole, or perhaps even a wormhole.

The Tab is linked to the neural network headpiece he currently wears, placed there by external robotic arms, also under his control. His thoughts are giving directions rapidly which are transferred from one to the other and back for him to readily receive the data when it arrives.

The probe, having successfully endured its faster-than-light route, has dropped back into regular space and now approaches the foreign object, sensors at full capacity. Varez is astounded. They read nothing, yet he plainly sees the black thing through the viewscreen. He decides obtaining a sample is in order. He orders the probe to extend an arm and scoop up whatever it can. It performs the procedure perfectly. The readings are mystifying, still showing an absence of anything yet the container is now back within the probe, clearly showing that there is something inside it. Varez decides to take a distant reading. He verifies the neural network is ready to receive data. He orders the robotic arm to reach into the container, touch the material and relay the readings back to him.

He feels a surge through the system; something foreign is finding its way into the neural network. How is that even possible at such a distance? Due to his mutation, he doesn't normally feel sensations like others, but he does this time. Something is trying to move from the headgear into him. Something that does not feel like a cute, cuddly alien. He has contingencies in place for just such an occurrence. He shuts the headgear and all systems down, disconnecting everything. He purges the system and repeatedly runs multi-level system diagnostics through the night. He blows up the Explorer just to be safe. That will take some explaining.

In the morning everything reads clear. Whatever it was, it is gone. So wrong! It lingers in the background, in the wiring, in the electrical impulses. It seeks to learn.

When Varez next puts on the helmet, he finds himself overtaken. It happens so slowly, that initially he does not realize what is happening. The thing is sly, careful, cautious. Undetectable at first, once he recognizes it, he knows it is too late to simply purge the system again. It is trying to breach his mind now, but he is a force to be reckoned with. A genius with an IQ beyond most mortals. He will not give in without a fight.

He theorized for a long time that there might be multiple realities. Some kind of duplication that branched off based on significant events or focal points in people's lives. Maybe he has duplicates across multiple universes, just as smart as him or even smarter. It was going to be his next project.

He had even started to build a rudimentary communications array to see if it was possible to communicate across space to different realities. A possibility? A last resort before the invasive creature subjugates his mind completely. His hands fly over the Tab, activating the test array. He cannot speak, he lost that ability long ago, but his thoughts are communicated through the neural net via the Tab which vocalizes them and sends them out through the array. He has no idea if it will work or even if anyone will ever hear it.

But something else happens to bolster his confidence. In his mental struggle with the creature, he discovers a gift. Perhaps it is because he has not been able to use his voice for so long. Suddenly he becomes aware of it. Telepathy. Mind and thought projection. The ability is there. He believes he can use this mixture of previously untapped telepathic ability and combine it with his understanding of science and technology to amplify the message's broadcast.

He must try. Just as the creature started learning from him, he learns from It. What It is about, what Its purpose is, Its Mission, the danger It poses. He communicates all of this in his message, not knowing if it went anywhere at all. It is bent on destroying everything and everyone. The antithesis of life, It will swallow all that is and leave a void where all of existence used to be. Everything will be devoid of life, until only It is left. A deep dark Abyss. It is some kind of Devoid. A Devoid that is coming for everything. Perhaps someone out there will hear or even respond.

Finally, he makes the only move he conceivably has left. If he can't purge the system, he will purge himself and the entity along with it. At the very least, he will no longer be of interest to It. He knows the risk, but he refuses to allow It into his world. He sends a unique self-destruct signal through the Tab. The message is relayed through every device, including the neural net headgear he wears. Everything fries, including his brain. When they find him after a time, he is alive, but nothing more than a vegetable, his intellect lost in a black hole.

Varez's message floats out into The All, spreading across realities through time and space. Lingering. Seeking. Drifting. Searching for like minds. For counterparts, copies, variations. For any others who will be able to receive and understand. The Devoid may have been pushed away from this sentient's world, but It uses the message to Its advantage. Its tendrils follow the projected transmission everywhere as it spreads throughout all the variations within The All.

Across the entirety of The All, there is only a considerably small margin of sentients capable of theorizing the idea of a multiple number of versions of original universes. Even then, most of them can only take the idea so far before their minds begin to fracture at the immensity of such a concept. A small few like Varez can take the next step, a leap into the unknown, an unfathomable mystery that beckons to be solved. Varez may have provided salvation for many, though he will never know it.

A world mourns its genius. An entity learns. A Guardian laments.

A thread damaged.

Interlude – Named

A previous encounter with a powerful biological has been both rewarding and disturbing. Unexpected success and failure. It had not yet been exposed to such a strong force of will. Never forced out like that. Even the thing, the persona, that previously tried to force It to reveal Itself had not been able to stand against Its dark will and was driven away. It sensed that had been an even greater being, so how odd that this minuscule sentient had successfully resisted.

Yet success too; so much information. It absorbed it all at once. Such intelligence. It fed that into Itself. Processed. Discerned. Intellect. Growth. Expansion. Critical thought. Understanding. Full Self-Awareness.

And a name. Before the being's threat was eliminated, it had cried out a name. The term was familiar, perhaps the being had picked it up from the creature's own evolving thought patterns. It bounced the appellation all around and through Its massive being. Tested it out. Tasted it. Agreed. Smiled inwardly. It liked it. Self-Awareness. Sentience. Now a name for Itself: The Devoid.

On Its journey to annihilate all life and leave nothing but Itself, The Devoid will absorb all from everywhere and everything. The concept is thoroughly pleasing. The name and understanding resonate within Its dark core of raw, lustful, unending hunger.

Sustenance for an eternity. Maybe even infinity. An intelligent laugh.

The Devoid.

The barefoot eight-year-old little girl with wavy, blond hair thinks about picture books, and the nice old man and the interesting lady who use to read to her when she was in a bed. Somewhere.

They wore such funny clothes.

She keeps walking on her way to meet Someone.

Someone who needs her.

Someone important who needs her very much.

CHAPTER FOUR

Variations On a Theme – Andante

The musical term andante is an indication to play or sing music with a relaxed, natural and moderate tempo, a light, flowing rhythm.

Lindsay – Sunset

Lindsay Ballinger watches the sunset over the eastern horizon, her feet cooling off in the small evening waves as she stands in the water just a little way in from shore. The sun glows a fierce red as it begins to set. *"Red sky at night, sailor's delight."* She smiles at the thought of the old saying. She has come to contemplate her future. Her parents kindly rented a cottage for her at one of her favourite beaches for part of the summer. It's a wonderful graduation present.

She completed her studies with highest honours, joint master's degrees in science and linguistics. It's an odd combination, but each discipline helped her understand the other more thoroughly. Now the future beckons and decisions are required. Not too hastily though, there is still lots of time. A PhD? Dentistry? Medicine? A break for a year, maybe travel? What about the guy she is sort of dating? Are they even on the same page? Marriage? So much to consider. Lost in thought, she stares at the sun's last glimmer as it disappears below the horizon.

She wants to accomplish something significant, something that will make a difference. Do something that will help change the world for the better, or at least make a positive change in whatever corner of the world she finds herself. It's what her family has modelled for her and the desire comes naturally. She knows she won't be satisfied or happy if she does not at least try.

"Go! Now!"

What was that? An inner voice? Outer voice? Did someone say something? She looks around, her reverie broken. No one there. Perhaps her own intuition. Is she becoming delusional?

It comes again, stronger than before, "Leave now! Hurry!"

Whatever it is, she now feels very unsafe. Perhaps it is her intuition. No hesitation now. She takes off for the cottage. Once there, she locks the door, makes sure all the windows are shut and locked down. She calls her parents to check in and then calls her boyfriend. Can she call him a boyfriend yet? She calls him regardless. She feels relieved and safe.

A dark hooded figure, serrated knife in hand, emerges from underneath a dock on the beach, situated slightly farther down from where Lindsay stood only moments before. He is certain there had been someone there. He walks over to where he thought the woman had been standing but sees no one. It is too dark to track footprints and all he sees are shadows of a mishmash of multiple barefoot imprints overlaying each other in every direction. He pockets the knife, deciding to seek a victim to satisfy his unholy addiction elsewhere in the dark of the beach.

On this eighth planet of its solar system, one with a retrograde rotation, within the 666,011,101st galaxy, about 1,959 universes away from one of its counterparts, Lindsay contemplates the fragility of life and its briefness. Yes, something significant is her life's calling. Whatever shape that might take, she has yet to determine.

No one mourns. Something fumes. A Guardian rejoices.
A thread continues.

Interlude – Strategic

The Nexus perceives something unnatural has been happening out on the fringes. Something tampering with pathways. More than a few pools gone dry, mirrors darkened, maze doors vanished. One or two over ages of time, perhaps a curiosity. More than that in a short time, likely only coincidence. Now though, this many so close together, within such a short time span as some sentients might measure it, it's definitely a concern. A pattern emerges. Potents! Those with possible unique destinies are being hunted everywhere across The All. Not random. Deliberate. A goal of extinction. The hunter is no longer subtle. The hunter tracks. The hunter now hurries. Why? An unknown.

An Unnamed. A threat. A dark thread yet invisible. The Nexus waits.

*   *   *   *

The Devoid understands even more keenly now, that specific biologicals pose a threat. The ones with life threads that beat at a different rhythm and glow a different hue. It does not know what to call them yet and It does not care. It just knows they must be eliminated. If their destinies could do It harm, they must be stopped. It understands how to track them. Use the different routes and pathways found during Its instinctive experimentation phase. It will methodically and strategically search out all the targets, carefully, cautiously, subtly bringing an end to any threat they pose to Its ongoing existence. Feed. Destroy. Eliminate. If needed, It will swallow an entire galaxy or universe along the way, to achieve Its goal. A dual purpose. Misdirection and gratification both.

THE FIFTH GUARDIAN: A SYMPHONY OF DISCORD

The Devoid strategizes. The Guardians contemplate.
Potents in the crosshairs. Threads hang in the balance.

Bran'Os Ty – Determined

On this wet twenty-third day of the fifth month, Bran'Os Ty's rocky troll form stands stoically in the torrential rain. Angry. Frustrated. Soaked. Fatigued. Thousands and thousands of light years from it, his is the sole planet orbiting a quasar in a galaxy within a universe, that for those who measure time, is one of the most ancient, its origins very early on in the path of creation.

Perhaps that is why some of the sentients on the planet, like Bran'Os', have the use of magic. Their scientists theorize that it has more to do with the black hole and the quasar around which their world spins. Irrelevant. If the scientists had left well enough alone, his world wouldn't be in this mess. His sister would still be alive.

It was a tenacious compromise at first, a new strategic alliance. A world where magic and science have reached an understanding. A balance, a fragile agreement to work together, especially now, considering what has happened. The reason for Bran'Os' anger. Well, part of the reason.

The scientists, eager to learn, but unlearned in magic, think it's simply science they do not yet understand. They are determined. They see so much potential good in its use, and combined with the technology they do know, dream of making a better world. Bran'Os knows better; magic is more than just science, it will always be like that. The scientists are only partially right; there is a sort of science to it, but it also requires something deep from one's soul to work properly, to be effective, to be useful. Something deep inside that will also be costly.

The scientists went too far. Combining magic and science before they were ready, they managed to open an inter-dimensional gateway. What came out of it, no one could have predicted. Bran'Os thought maybe he could have, but no one had asked his opinion.

The demon hordes from another dimension poured out and upon their planet in a wild rage, destroying everything in their path. His civilization had no other word to describe the beings, other than demon. Perhaps they are sentient, but if so, they don't act like it. More like wild animals imprisoned for longer than should be allowed, any form of intelligence long departed. The incursions continued until magic and science allied together, killed them off or forced those remaining back through the gate. An impenetrable force shield, created by magic and science combined is put into place and holds. The planet's inhabitants breathe a sigh of relief, relax and go back to what is left of normal, rebuilding what is lost.

Not all could be rebuilt. Not Bran'Os's sister, who perished in the first invasion wave. Now he stands in the fierce rain, living it all over again. The idiots! The scientists, who always think themselves smarter, have meddled again. They couldn't leave well enough alone. They thought to improve the shield that held the gateway closed. Instead, their lack of understanding of the true nature of magic, resulted in a breach and the eventual collapse of the barrier. They feel bad. They apologize. Bran'Os wants to dissolve them into nothingness.

His magic is that powerful, but he also needs them. If they are going to be victorious, they must work together. This time though, Bran'Os Ty oversees everything. The building of weapons and their infusion with magic by the wielders he has carefully trained. Deployment. Strategy. Command of the forces. He is part of it all. He made sure he would be. He owes his sister at least that.

He stands with the largest force, waiting for the next onslaught. He senses the demons regrouping. They did not do well the first time and were pushed back. Bran'Os recognizes that some, but not all of the attacks across his world are different than the original wave of insanity. Purpose.

Stratagem. Organization. Something sorely lacking the very first time they fell upon his world.

He morphs his troll form so he can drop to the ground on all fours, a unique capability that nature has granted some of his race. Not magic, simply a quirk of evolution. He sniffs the air and the ground. He sends a light-feeler through the rain across to where he knows the enemy gathers. The magical element returns to tell him more. Something there. Something different. Unbelievable.

He rises, resuming his craggy troll form and shouts to the gathered forces above the driving rain. He could have eliminated the downpour with his magic but thinks they may use the slippery ground to their advantage, nor does he wish to drain himself prematurely. Lately, it takes longer for his soul to recharge. Not like when he was younger. He signals to indicate their enemy is on the move. Before he finishes, the horde appears, scrambling madly forward. Oddly, they seem oblivious to the force in front of them, like they are intentionally running to their doom. No strategy this time, just chaos.

Bran'Os turns towards the forces holding the larger, most deadly weapons and summons the magic. He wraps its glow within his hands and then hurls it into the deadly projectiles, infusing them with extra layers of power. Power enough to cut down massive amounts of insurgents. It has to be. The number of demons racing towards them is more than they have ever encountered.

Not completely drained, it will take some time before he crosses that line, he motions to his compatriots and summons the magic again along with his other magic-wielders. This is the first volley, designed to slow the advance. Next, on his order, the atom-splitting projectiles, now infused with indomitable, superior magic, will be unleashed and decimate everything in front of them. At least, that is the plan.

Bran'Os senses it again and he suddenly understands: these demons are not running *to,* they are running *from.* Something. Something behind them. He reaches out, sending the magic past and above their crazed foes, towards the breach in the gateway. Something hidden. A force. No, something intelligent. Devious. Hungry. A formidable will. Whatever it is, it is sentient.

Too caught up attempting to discern the nature of the hidden thing, he fails to notice how close the demons are. Panic. He hasn't yet signaled for deployment of the larger weapons. Fools! They should have just done it. If fired now, so close to their lines, both sides will be caught up in the decimation. No choice. He signs them to launch. His forces look at him in terror but understand. It is done.

Bran'Os, along with his magic-wielders, cast up as much of a barrier as they can to protect as many as possible. Some survive, the rest, both demons and trolls, destroyed. Bran'Os survives. It isn't over though, he knows that. There is still Something. Some evil back there, frightening and powerful enough to scare the demons. On the other side of the gateway or perhaps already through.

He has enough within him to send one last piece of seeking magic through. If he can identify the nature of the creature before it is too late, perhaps they won't have to live through another war. The inquiring magic returns. He opens his weary mind and his worn hands to receive it.

He needs to examine it. Wait! Wrong colour! It is tainted. Something has malformed it. Corrupted it. Already in his hands, it burns. It fills his rock-hard craggy troll body with agonizing pain. He tries to shut it down, summons all the magic left within him. Maybe science would have helped. It is enveloping him, from the inside out. *"Fool! You should have paid more attention!"* he reproaches himself. His fellows look on in despair. His body implodes. The corrupted magic then explodes from within him, propelling rocky, pebble-like fragments everywhere. The most powerful magic wielder on the planet, Bran'Os Ty, dies that day. No one is sure why.

Magic and science mourn. A Guardian winces. A malignancy learns.
A thread shatters.

Matos Jason – Concord

In a very elderly universe, in an almost equally aged galaxy, Matos Jason tracks the thieves from above. High up and out of sight, they miss seeing him fly overhead, but his far-sight vision tells him their current position and the direction they head in. They are aiming for the spaceport. Likely to steal a shuttle and secure themselves in their hidden base on one of the planet's moons. Not so hidden though, as Jason has already determined the base's location. He could intercept them, forcing the shuttle back to the ground, but chooses a different strategy.

He needs to find out the identity of their silent partner and though he suspects who it is, he wants confirmation before making any accusations or arrests. After all, that's what made him the best law enforcement officer on the planet. Still, he is unable to shake the feeling that there is something more significant in play. His heightened instincts tell him so, but what that might be remains a mystery.

Now that his civilization has developed space travel, at least within their own solar system, they have encountered other species with whom they share the system. Not all of them are law-abiding either. First contact is still a very new experience for many of the races, though they are slowly growing accustomed to the concept.

It quickly became apparent, that unlike Matos Jason's home world, none of the other sentient life forms in their solar system have evolved with enhanced abilities. Not all their first contacts were thrilled to discover how ordinary they were in comparison. A seed for jealousy and fear. Some viewed Jason's people as a threat, not understanding that they are a peaceful race.

There are exceptions of course; not all of Jason's race treats their abilities with respect. There are a minority who seek to do harm, or use their gifts for nefarious purposes, however, after many tough lessons learned, proactive measures, such as the power nullifiers he helped create, were put in place long ago, to inhibit such behaviour and when necessary, rehabilitate appropriately.

Since meeting others with whom they shared the system, rumours run rampant about disappearances of his people. Whispers of genetic testing, unorthodox experiments, sometimes resulting in brain damage or death. All in an effort by some of their neighbours to give themselves the same enhancements. Nothing is proven yet. This is the case assigned to Matos Jason.

Using his far-sight, he scans the interior of the cargo containers and the ships at the spaceport. Nothing. His augmented senses react before it happens, his instincts create a force field around himself as a hail of nullifiers come at him from multiple directions. A blur speeds by. The shooting ceases. He acknowledges the work of the speedster with a nod.

He sees the shuttle fly out of the space port, cloaks himself from view and causes his body to vibrate at rotating frequencies to confuse any sensor scans. Flying upwards, he contacts both Control and his life partner, letting them know the mission is taking him off-world.

He passes through the exosphere, the shuttle still in sight. Activity to his left catches his attention. Is that a black hole? No. Impossible. But something. A fissure breaks open in space, the gravity exerting tremendous force, pulling him towards its expanding opening. Even with his powers, he cannot resist the intense pull and begins tumbling towards its maw.

He contacts Control to warn them. His message bounces back like an echo. The same when he tries his partner. He attempts more conventional means, using his backup, an older hand-held transmitter. Only static. He continues careening towards the opening. Every effort to fly in the other direction is futile.

At the edge of his vision, he notices something foreign, out of place. He concentrates enough to use his far-sight. There is a creeping wave sweeping across the system, leaving nothing in its wake. How can that be? The entire system blinks out. Maybe the whole galaxy. He only sees an empty void where everything had once been. He screams in anger, succumbing to the pull of the wormhole and vanishes within it.

A maliciousness is pensive. A Guardian frowns. Matos Jason mourns. A thread glows.

Interlude – Potents

Scattered across the infinite number of universes and varied worlds within The All, there have always been Potents. No matter the time, era, or rise and fall of civilizations, there are always Potents. The number of them vary, but always sentient beings, though race, species, worlds and universes always differ.

The powers of Creation have insisted and seen fit to ensure their existence across all times and places. Not always the same individuals. As the existing ones age out, new ones are found and designated. Whether this is the doing of the Nexus, The All, or a combination thereof, or from a different Source remains unknown. Sufficient to simply say, the Potents are always there, to be called on should the need arise.

The Potents do not know of this at all. They are simply sentient beings living out their lives whatever that may look like. They have no idea of what being a Potent means, or that they have been selected to be such, or that they may be called upon if The All is in a time of need, or what that time of need may even be or look like. Their possible destiny is a complete mystery to them.

Though the Potents themselves are unaware, there is one aspect that does stand out, revealing who they are to discerning sight. The threads of their lives glow a unique hue of amber, and those life threads vibrate at a rate that is unique only to them. Identifiers that will allow the Guardians to seek, track and find them. Something less benevolent has also discovered that fact.

The Potents live their lives. The Guardians seek them.
Something Dark hunts them too.

Reb – Fatal

In a not-so-obscure galaxy, Reb, short for Rebel, expertly pilots her starship through the mine fields while her crew holds their collective breath. They are on another run to extricate some wrongly accused prisoners and unfortunate children from the transport vessel flying them to the work prison on the smallest moon of the system's fifth planet.

She has not told the crew that this is likely her last mission. She feels the disease intensely and is certain it now spreads through her whole body. Damn thing! Nothing to be done; this one has no known cure. A rare contagion she probably picked up from one of the alien races they barter with to keep their ship running. She needs the ship to always be in top condition so they can keep rescuing the unfortunates who fall into the Slaver's Union's sights and their inequitable system of so-called justice. *"Justice. Ha! More like, 'Just an excuse to get more slaves.'"*

Reb knows that well. Her parents mysteriously disappeared when she was eleven cycles old and she found herself taken in by a supposedly well-meaning family. It wasn't long before she was sold to the Slaver's Union, where she discovered the harsh realities of being nothing more than a piece of property. She was traded many times, until one master found her skilled with engineering, navigation and piloting. He used her at his pleasure and she became part of his raiding parties, capturing more innocents to become slaves of whomever the Union could sell their new acquisitions to.

By the time she reached sixteen cycles, her rebellious spirit kicked in full throttle. She led a very successful mutiny along with other enslaved teens and some disgruntled crew that no longer cared much for their leader. That is how the name Rebel, or Reb, stuck. She had long ago forgotten it used to be Rebecca. Now she is driven by her mission to free as many as she possibly can before… She thought she would be doing the work for a long time. Now, that does not seem probable.

Her pain comes in waves, off and on. Up until this point, she has been able to hide it from most of her crew. Only her mate and her son know of her situation and they promised to keep it quiet. They are both quite capable of taking over for her when she is gone.

Her thoughts return to the situation at hand. One last major rescue is how she wants to finish things off and then go off to a pretty little planet they once visited on their travels and settle down there with her mate and son for whatever time she has left. Her crew will get to take a well-deserved, permanent break wherever they want.

Another wave of pain fills her body, then subsides as they approach the transport ship, their shielding and cloak in place. She imagines the grateful looks on the people they are about to rescue once they are all safely onboard her ship. She gives the order to proceed: disable the transport ship's engines and shields, scan for the correct life signs and beam them into their own cargo bay. Then get the hell out of this area of space as fast as the light drive will take them. Simple. Straightforward. Routine. Until it isn't.

A blackness starts to engulf one end of the Union's ship, just as they were about to transport the prisoners on to their own vessel. The other ship rocks and fires, trying to get away from whatever holds it immobile. Her crew tells her the scanners are not picking anything up, even though they all can see what is happening through their own viewscreen.

Determined not to lose the prisoners, Reb orders weapons control to fire on the black thing to force it off the transport ship. The blackness absorbs their weapons fire; it has no effect at all. Instead, the thing spits it out at the transport ship, disintegrating it. The bridge of Reb's ship goes utterly silent. She thinks of all those children, gone in an instant. She has failed.

Furious, she orders everything the ship has fired at the black shape. In response, it heads towards them. Waves of pain soars through her body. *Not now. Please not now!* The crew watch her grow pale and then faint. They call for her mate and son. By the time they arrive, the black thing has already begun to swallow Reb's ship. It is too late for her. She is gone. It is too late for them. They will all be dead in a matter of moments.

The freed mourn. A Guardian is surprised. A hunger satisfied.
A thread dissolves.

Interlude – Awareness

The pillars of protection, the portals weakened by the continuous subtle onslaught over time, of the efforts to infiltrate Chaos and Order, to subsume all created within The All. To challenge the existence of The All itself, threatening to consume it into total blackness. If It finds Its way to the Nexus, It could attempt such a thing.

The Guardians know. The Guardians must restore the balance before the darkness becomes rampant and starts charging unchecked, enveloping The All in Its thick blackness of nothingness. The Guardians know what must be done, the Guardians must reach out, the Guardians must seek. The Voice has told them. As much as there is only one explanation, there is now only one solution. The Guardians must seek this solution as subtly and as warily as It found Its foothold in the first place.

The bifurcation points have been found by the Darkness. Those optimal focal points that could lead in so many different directions, in so many different universes, depending on choices made and the consequences that may ensue. Those hinges where destinies could take so many different directions. The alternatives lived out, the time line bisected, trisected, the point where Time Space Eternity Infinity meet in a unique blending where Destiny could be realized or nullified and all come to naught.

The strategy becomes clearer over the ages of time. The darkness seeks out these places. In the multiverse, in all the alternative universes, it is what the creature seeks. Seeking to infiltrate, seeking to prevent, seeking to push the decisions in directions for nullification of all Potents. Instinct, will, pure malevolence, an indomitable force. The darkness seeks out places where Life, Death and Destiny teeter on what would happen within, weaken the barriers, find Its prey. Void everything. Harbinger of emptiness, gloom, despair and everything that sustains It and feeds Its insatiable appetite.

No longer Nameless. The Devoid stalks Its prey.
The Guardians race against the blackness.

Tavarez – Solitary

Sometimes within universes, whether originals or replicants, the energies involved in evolution, creation and new iterations of being, spring forth rather surprising and unpredictable results. It is in one of these variations, a universe well above the one quintillionth mark within The All, where in the midst of its galaxies, life evolved and populated rapidly on a small planet, second in order from its sun. Not unusual and quite often inevitable, at some point along the way in these evolutionary processes, a mutation occurs.

How awful to be the only one who cannot hear the voices. The single one among your people unable to project your thoughts or receive those of others. Never to experience the sensation of the visions or hear the mysterious voices that come to everyone else. To be an oddity.

This is the case for Tavarez. His parents grew concerned, when at an early age he did not show the same ability as his peers, unable to hear the voices, see the visions, experience the healthy paranoia. The doctors in those days simply said he was a late bloomer and that in time these gifts would come. Yet they never have. By the time Tavarez is an adolescent, it is obvious to everyone that he is different. Not only is he incapable of projecting his thoughts to them, they cannot project theirs through to him. It is akin to hitting an invisible wall. This only made his situation worse.

The mocking, the jeers, the teasing comes from all kinds of people, except for a few compassionate, understanding souls. The best solution for him seems to be self-inflicted isolation. It is the only way to deal with the rejection. There are certainly times when the depression is overwhelming, the sense of persecution, the loneliness, unbearable. Times when thoughts of ending the pain by taking his life are not that far off but something always restrains him. The thought of the hurt it would cause his parents, even though he feels he has caused them more than enough grief already, make it an unwelcome answer.

Something more holds him back as well: a sense that there must be a reason, some other purpose for what some call a disability. If that is true, he hopes one day it will show itself. He is impatient and if a purpose does not manifest itself soon, he has plans to leave. Not to die by his own hand, not yet at least, but to leave. Leave his peoples and trek elsewhere, to explore the world. Maybe even one day during his travels, out of the blue, suddenly, unexpectedly, the gifting will appear, and then he will be like everyone else. He dreams a lot of that day. Though even in his dreaming, the fantasy never seems to completely unfold that way, at least the part about being like everybody else.

The medical community has studied him, administered so many drugs to correct his imperfections he wonders now if they are part of the problem rather than the solution. Many people whisper that he has become an addict like some of the other rebels.

Through self-medication of illegal pharmaceuticals, there are those, naming themselves rebels, who have chosen to dampen their perceptive abilities. They no longer wish their thoughts crowded with those of others, or to hear random voices from whatever their source, or allow their own minds exposed so freely.

They have become outcasts. Ironically Tavarez can relate. His status of outcast is because of his natural condition, theirs self-induced, either way, the result is the same. Shunned, ridiculed, an embarrassment to family, friends and pretty much everyone else.

The future looks bleak. The past haunted. The present a mix of both. Tavarez decides leaving is the best option. A time to find himself. A journey of self-discovery. His family does not even try to dissuade him; they feel for him but he is as much of a mystery to them as he is to himself. Wherever the journey will take him, it is better than staying. Something new. Something different. *"Different. How well I know that word,"* he reflects as he packs up, his parents and siblings watching, hesitantly offering to help. They don't want to make it seem as though they are happy to be rid of him. Maybe they are, maybe not. Tavarez understands.

They provide him with lots of food, supplies and funds. That is nice. He knows they love him, but this is hard for all of them; his life has made it that way. He hates what his life, his disability, has done to them, perhaps more so than what it has done to him. He hugs his fuzzy four-legged Dookery, supposed to be the family pet, but more so his than anyone else's; one of his best friends from early on and maybe the only family member that truly understands him. He reassures the loving creature that he will return soon and instructs it to look after the family in his absence.

He says his farewells and heads towards the piece of geography on his planet that has always aroused his curiosity: the mountains. He has never climbed one but has thought about it though. They are daunting. Why not? Alone in the wilderness, no one to see him if he doesn't do it correctly. It is worth the risk. He doesn't even know if he has the right gear for such a feat. He is determined. He will climb in his bare hands and bare feet if it means accomplishing something. Something for himself. No one else matters out here.

He finds a place to purchase supplies for the task. It is obvious to the shopkeeper that Tavarez has never done this before. He is supportive but cautious. Warns him of the pitfalls. When he realizes Tavarez is going to do this solo, he is disturbed and anxious. He attempts to project the dangers of that idea into Tavarez's mind but hits a wall. That bothers the shopkeeper more than the idea of Tavarez climbing alone.

He dissuades Tavarez from climbing the tallest peak and suggests, for a novice, the fourth or fifth in the group are a good starting place. Tavarez wants to tackle at least the second or third highest. They compromise on the third. The shopkeeper, still thrown by Tavarez's lack of normal communicative ability and his focused determination, moves things along.

For the chosen target, he provides maps, explains the paths, the ascents and the lack of oxygen as one climbs higher. He describes the best sites to stop, rest and acclimatize to the less breathable air. He also provides a brief tutorial on how to use the gear. Tavarez wishes he had taken notes. He remembers less than half of what he was told; there was so much information. The store keeper wishes he had never encountered the young man. He is positive he is sending him to his death.

After a restful sleep, Tavarez starts early, beginning his climb as the sun rises in the background, broadcasting its early morning rays. It happens on the third ascent, with two more to go. Tavarez witnesses a life-changing view of what lies before him and a clear vision of his destination. It makes him even more determined to achieve his goal. Until *it* happens.

He is a quarter of the way up, when he hears a voice. Hears it in his head, in his mind, not externally. At first, he thinks it is the shopkeeper, because the impression of the words were along the lines of, *"I see you are making good progress, Tavarez."* He knows from listening to others, that when hearing a voice internally, it will sound the same as the projecting person's voice. In that case, the voice is definitely not that of the shopkeeper.

He hears the voice repeat the same phrase again, this time with such a sarcastic tone, he thinks it is mocking him. He ignores it and continues his climb. It comes back louder again. Loud enough this time that it shakes him both mentally and physically.

Originally, he was excited to hear the voice, thinking that finally the gifting had arrived. Now he feels uncomfortable. The voice is ragged, scratchy, edgy, making his skin crawl. Why can he hear it? He tries to block it, but does not have the skills or experience to do so. His attention focused on defensiveness, he forgets where he is and what he is doing.

He loses both handholds and footholds simultaneously. His rope holds, swinging precariously, suspending him between rocks, ledges and the mountains. He doesn't have enough experience to know what to do. He is all alone except for the voice. He can hear it in his mind laughing at him, taunting him. His eyes well up with tears. There is only open sky above him, and the deadly ground far below, waiting patiently to receive him. The rope, buffeted by an increasing wind, sways to and fro, a helpless and hopeless Tavarez still attached. He tries to reach out, to call for help with his mind. Nothing, just the usual dead air. He closes his eyes and waits.

No one yet knows to mourn. A voice snickers. A Guardian waits.
A thread hangs.

The barefoot eight-year-old little girl with wavy, blond hair and a wonderful smile thinks about picture books, and the nice old man and the interesting lady who use to read to her when she was in a bed somewhere. They wore such funny clothes. She keeps walking on her way to meet Someone.

Someone who needs her.

Someone very, very important who needs her.

CHAPTER FIVE

Variations On a Theme –Discord

Discord is a combination of musical sounds that strikes the ear harshly with unpleasant sounds of dissonance.

Lindsay – Dusk

It had not been that long since she made sure her teens were in bed when Lindsay Felger hears the noise downstairs. She recognizes it as glass breaking, a door opening and then voices coming from her office. The sounds of low whispering, and the word *"safe,"* float through the air. She rushes to the kids' bedrooms and ushers them quickly into the panic room. She ensured there was one in place after the last go 'round when she had become the catalyst that changed her world.

Lindsay is a medical researcher, a prodigy, wunderkind level. Like so many scientific discoveries in the history of her world, hers was purely accidental. She was trying to solve a unique medical problem, a rare fatal disease that afflicts a minority of the population, but significant enough that the numbers have started rising. The number included her husband. His loss fuels her motivation to get it right for the next family. She starts experimenting with a compound that might actually cause the disease to recess, perhaps even dissolve. The compound has rather unique properties. After a great deal of testing, she concludes it will not work on the disease.

She notices something else about the compound though. After more study, experimentation, combining it with a few other substances and observing multitudes of chemical reactions, she discovers she was correct. She has found the substitute for fossil fuels. The thing that keeps her world moving, that provides the source of energy necessary for all forms of transportation on her planet. Both a blessing and a curse, fossil fuels keep everything moving, but they are also severely damaging the climate of the planet. There are already signs. There are many days prior to her discovery when she wonders if her children and grandchildren will even have breathable air by the time they are middle-aged. Her discovery revolutionizes her world.

A world in a solar system boasting twelve planets orbiting a trinary star. Terra, as they call it, is the eleventh planet in the system, far enough away that the massive heat from their triple suns is not overpowering and still allows life to flourish. Though if they keep going with the amount of pollution they continually pour into the air through their transportation system, the protective layers in the atmosphere will eventually deteriorate, leaving the planet a scorched shell. At least, so the theories say. How long before that happens is a matter of regular debate.

That all changes though when Lindsay changes the world. Accomplishes something significant as her parents always encouraged. *"Wherever you are, whatever you do, be sure to change your corner of the universe for the better."* She took the advice to heart. She doesn't expect her contributions would be that important, but this one is. With the change in the source of fuel, the climate begins to heal. Rapidly. The naysayers cannot argue against that one.

She is praised and lauded all around the globe. A Nobellity Prize. Accolades and offers galore. Every research firm on the planet is offering her massive grants worth sums of money she only dreams of, if she will come on board and do the research they want her to. Of course, not everyone is happy about what happened, particularly, the fossil fuel companies and their associated subsidiaries.

At first they offer her money to not reveal her discovery. As in huge sums of currency and extra benefits. Then they try to block her patent. Then negative stories in the press, declaring her find a fraud. When that doesn't work, other more devious means are employed. Intimidating her by following her or her children, sending her pictures of the kids showing they are tracking their movements. Law enforcement soon puts a stop to that. Still, there are times when she feels like she is being followed and not by the good guys. That is when she has the panic room installed. Just a precaution.

The opposition eventually gives up. They can't deny the climate has drastically improved. Embarrassed, but not deterred, they turn their energies back to making profit. They retool all their manufacturing plants, their partners do the same across the globe. They design newer machines and factories to produce vehicles that will run on the new compound. They create depot stations that will sell it. Bottom line, they still make their billions in profit. And the planet's climate continues to heal.

Lindsay motions the kids to be quiet, indicating she is going downstairs to have a look. They try to dissuade her. Her youngest, at fifteen, wants to come with her to protect her. She orders him to be the man and look after his older seventeen-year-old sister. He might need to protect her.

She goes down and surprises the intruders. Scattered papers are strewn across her office. Her safe open, vials pulled out and smashed. It is a mess. Her arrival startles them. They panic. She grabs a lamp and throws it at one of them. It hits him, but not enough to make an impact.

One of them grabs the crowbar they used to pry open the safe and smashes it across her head. She falls to the floor in pain. He hits her in the skull a few more times for good measure. All she can think of through the pain, is her children are without their last parent, and who will carry on her research? She is so close. The cure for cancer, one test away.

Originally the invaders' instructions were to collect what research they could, anything that looked important, destroy the rest, and then burn the house down. Fortunately for Lindsay and the kids, they were too surprised by her appearance to follow through. They take off their masks, their faces beaded in sweat, discuss what they should do and then run out of the house. After all, they destroyed what they could and the bitch was dead anyway, so no more research. They don't know about all the video monitors throughout the house Lindsay had installed when she had the panic room built.

The kids upstairs open the panic room door just enough to listen when they hear the commotion stop. The are scared and argue about whether to go down and help their mother or wait. The son wants to run down, but fearing for his safety, his sister pulls him back. They secure the panic door and wait until morning. Neither sleep.

In the early hours, they open the door again. Nothing. Their mom has not returned to them. They are scared. They go down and find her on the floor, blood pooled, large contusions and swelling in the back of her head. She is still breathing. They call the emergency response services. Lindsay is rushed to the hospital, scanned and emergency surgery is employed. She has abrasions, possibly brain damage, an internal brain bleed and it is hemorrhaging. Surgery is successful. The children, now with both of Lindsay's parents present for support, are told she is alive.

However, things are different. She has lost a great deal of motor control in parts of her body, and worse, her intellect, that great mind of hers, will not be the same. She will not be able to think the same way, certainly not do research like she had before. Her thought processes are limited by damage to her cerebral cortex and misfiring neurons. She might be able to verbally communicate at some level, eventually, though it will be more at the mentality of a two-year-old. Maybe a three-year-old, if lucky. The damage is severe. Her intellect, intelligence, whatever the name for it, is gone and will never return. What a tragic loss. They will never know what other significant world and life-changing discoveries she would have made.

The world that she had impacted, literally saved, is furious. It comes together and provides her and the children with all the support possible. They want to ensure they at least have a comfortable life and that Lindsay will be well cared for, no matter how long she has to live.

Law enforcement from all over the globe work together to investigate. They identify the men using the video from Lindsay's house. Under the threat of death by lethal injection, the perpetrators flip on their bosses. A consortium of five large pharmaceutical companies who make huge profits from their production of drugs to treat cancer, along with three large firms that manufacture equipment to aid in its treatment are all found guilty. The CEO's and senior managers are put in jail for life.

Those companies go bankrupt when one of Lindsay's lab assistants finishes what she had started and finds the cure for cancer. He makes sure Lindsay receives all the credit. She has significantly impacted the world a second time, even if she can't understand it. The assistant insists she is on the platform with him when he receives the prize for this great accomplishment. Both her teens also become scientists. They are determined to follow in their mother's footsteps. They each want to do something significant too.

Sometime long after her injury, Lindsay feels something touch her mind. Even in her weakened, disabled state, she recognizes it is not something good. She feels the thing examining her. She can no longer articulate it, but if she could have, she would have said it was like arms of something reaching inside her, searching for something, scanning her mind. She has a vague recollection of how it was like when she ran a med-scanner over a man, her husband perhaps, a long time ago. The feeling leaves.

A world sorrows. A Violence elated. A Guardian troubled.
A thread immobilized.

Interlude - Fundamentals

"The space and time which I inhabit are in their different ways indeterminate horizons which contain various points of view. The synthesis of time like that of space is a task that always needs to be performed afresh."
M. Merleua-Ponty, Phénoménologie de la perception.

The Primal Forces of Space, Time, Infinity and Eternity are not so unrelated as some might believe. Intersectoral, actually. Boundless and boundary-less. In most Universes they function identically. With a few exceptions, including those peculiar one-off dimensions, their behaviour, their rules, what the sentients sometimes refer to as Laws, are always the same.

Even advanced races of sentients possess limited understanding of these forces, though they do have some inkling of how complex and yet beautifully simple each is in their various aspects. Except perhaps for Infinity and Eternity. Space-Time, as some of them have come to call it, is relatively easy in comparison to the other two forces. Those are beyond comprehension for most, a philosophical undertaking and debate for others, yet the Guardians have unlimited understanding of all of them. Not surprising, considering it is their mandate to guard them. To ensure they stay in balance. To safeguard the resulting Chaos and Order, which exist simultaneously throughout The All, continuing their constant flux guaranteeing the Four Forces operate in appropriate tandem and tension. This is the proper application of the equation which allows the symphony that is The All to play out Melody and Harmony in perfect balance and rhythm.

Although there are Four Guardians, they are not each assigned to an individual Force. There is no Guardian of Space and another one of Time.

Their combined consciousness abrogates that need. They are aware of each, both individually and corporately. Whether Eternity, Infinity, Space or Time, they simply know. Otherwise, how could they Guard? They feel a shift, an imbalance in any of them. Their ageless memories have no recollection of such a thing ever occurring.

Until now.

Bran – Descent

The waves resound with the cracks of thunder and flashes of lightning in a perfect harmony. Perfect at least to Bran. The clouds are black, thick and angry. The water is stirred in a constant tumult by the strong wind. He watches from the deck of his family cottage, wondering why he finds so much pleasure in watching this kind of storm. Observing it over the lake from a safe haven, both beautiful and threatening, calms his spirit and makes him feel at peace with the world, as ironic as that might sound. He raises one slanted eyebrow and muses how these storms he so enjoys are a violent chaotic scene with its own sense of calm.

He is fascinated by how this storm seems to draw him, even call to him to come closer. He leaves the safety of the deck and starts slowly walking towards the shore. The rain has not started yet, and he does not intend to stand close to the shore for long, after all, he needs to get back to his work. It is the reason he came alone. He hopes to accomplish a great deal without any distraction. He has made great progress but an interruption arrives.

He thinks he hears someone calling his name, but that is impossible. Probably the echo of the thunder over the lake playing tricks on him. No, there is his name again. Maybe family have come after all. Perhaps hearing of the storm, they are concerned. He turns back to see if there is anyone on the deck, but as he does, the downpour starts with such force, he barely sees in front of himself.

Ignoring the storm, Bran sheds his clothes and moves from the shore into the lake. The lightning is infrequent now, so little danger from the sky, hopefully. The sandbars extend out for a good length. He runs out on them until they are no more and then dives deep into the refreshing waters. He lets them bathe over his green-tinged skin, his gills now active.

On this glistening orb consisting of nine tenths green oceans, the energies of evolution and creation decided it made sense to create water-breathers who would become sentient. In fact, as it turns out, they are amphibious beings, capable of breathing both air and water, though for the most part, they prefer the water. The process took an immense amount of time, as the mostly green globe, ninth of ten planets, made its way slowly around its star, in what eventually Bran's people would refer to as cycles.

In the plethora of millions of galaxies in the universe it inhabited, its reality had been split off untold times over, into a series of replicants that only highly intelligent superior beings could track in terms of numbers and location.

Bran knows none of this, however he does enjoy a good swim. Like many of his kind, he loves to spend most of his time in the water, rather than on land. *Out sea,* or *land* as it is sometimes called, is for special times. Holy ceremonies, personal retreats, alone time away from the waves, lakes, seas and oceans and the millions of mer-people who inhabit them.

A school of harmless fish swim alongside him for a time. He laughs, relishing their uniqueness, and marvels at their multi-coloured variety. He swims out further to where the lake meets a larger body of water, the sea that he calls home. He emits a shrill sound unique to his familial ties. If his people have called his name, he will find out soon. He hears no response. He swims closer to home and tries again. Nothing. So odd. He swims faster, now worried something is amiss.

He is not wrong. The seabed is on fire, so are the dwellings. His home and others still burning. He looks up. Land-dwellers. Bloody creatures. They will pay. He calls repeatedly for each individual family member. No response. Finally, his sister answers, coming out of a hiding place among their old play area composed of rocks, seaweed and debris. She weeps uncontrollably. Their parents, friends, and neighbours are all kidnapped or have perished. Bran fumes, *"Why? So unfair!"*

He sees it before she does. A dagger, something the land people called a locator harpoon sent from up above. It can track and sense his people's presence. He pushes his sister out of the way and takes it full on in his chest. It bores itself all the way in and through, coming out his back. His bluish-green blood starts to smear and colour the water. His sister shrieks. She helps pull the thing out. He lies and tells her he will be fine, he just needs to rest. He instructs her to swim as fast as she can, to find all the remaining mer-people and rally them. He will find her. It was time to put an end to the air-breathers-only people on their planet. War will wage and they will be successful.

He watches her swim away. His sister is safe, at least for now. He prays to all the water-gods to protect her until she finds safe haven. He also begs them to strengthen his people as they wreak vengeance on the land-dwellers and to give them victory. His gills move their last, his body becomes light, his eyes dim and Bran floats away into the darkness and depths of his home world's many waters. His sister lives. Mourning will come later.

The mer-people war. A Guardian dismayed. A foulness applauds.

A thread descends.

Interlude - Failsafe

No matter what time period, from the very first universe to the most recent iteration, there is always a Failsafe within The All. The Nexus, whether through instinct or design, deemed it necessary to have such a thing embedded as a guarantee of protection, a bulwark against the remote possibility that at some time, itself or perhaps even the very existence of The All, might be threatened. Perhaps it was simply a natural mode of self-protection, or maybe through some foreshadowing it sensed across the ripples and waves of endless time, that it deigned in the grand symphonic scheme, such a pivotal piece was necessary.

Over the eons, the Failsafe has taken many shapes. A barely evolved animal life form. A bizarre one-of-a-kind creature from a particularly outlandish dimension. A quiet magical creation. A sentient being. A naturally occurring life-form of pure energy. As each passes through their lives and then moves beyond, the Nexus reaches out to find new versions. Through multiple millennia, all the variations of the Failsafe are many, but all hold the same purpose, a subtly hidden defence, able to be called upon should the unthinkable occur: The Nexus in danger, The All in great peril, the Guardians not enough.

The Nexus imbues some small part of itself within each version of the Failsafe. Perhaps The All does as well, however no Failsafe would ever know that or their true purpose. Their capability will only be revealed should the time come when their aid is required. Even then, they will be astounded at what is buried deep within themselves. Otherwise, every Failsafe throughout all Time, simply live out their existence until it is done, blissfully unaware of their potential and the unfathomable power they possess. Nor do they know their life threads vibrate at such a pace as to render their uniqueness mostly invisible. A unique hue, mostly untraceable.

The Voice knows. The Guardians aware. The Nexus knows.
The Devoid unsuspecting.

Jason – Combustion

A dozen universes over from its original, within a galaxy crowded by an unusually high number of stars, but fewer solar systems that could support life, in one of those few viable to do so, on the fourth planet circling its sun, a naked Jason Tomas wakes up to find he cannot move his legs.

His two favourite activities are his secret projects and sex with women. The first is about misdirection, manipulation and mitigation. Subtly taking over each crime syndicate in turn, making himself quite rich in the process. He accomplishes this behind the scenes, his identity a shadow. On the surface his motives are clearly about gaining power. Deeper, they are about tempering the level of violence, giving some relief to the poor souls who regularly suffer as collateral damage. Justification for his actions in a city already crumbling under the weight of its own avarice.

Last night's business was his second favourite activity. Handsome at six foot four, virile and ripe with pheromones, he has no time in his line of work for anything serious, no interest in relationships. He needs to guard his secrets. Random one-nighters are always the best option. Except last night's was not.

He can't get his mouth to form words and has no idea what is wrong. The woman he slept with, now sharply dressed, explains that after their fourth round of fun, she dropped a paralytic in the drink he asked for before he fell asleep.

She elaborates, explaining that meeting her is not a coincidence. She and her accomplices know his true identity and of his secret projects. The game is over. They are going to end him and take over themselves. Her friends are at his estate right now, tearing it apart, looking for proof. Her phone beeps and she bends over to show him the text message, *"Found everything we need."*

Jason's anger creates a surge of adrenaline reducing the effects of the paralytic. He manages to sit up, grab the woman by the hair and summon enough motor skills to pull her down and smash her face into his knee. She drops her cell.

Before she can recover from the shock, he grabs her phone and rapidly types the message, *"There's more to find. Keep looking."* Still enraged, he picks her up and hurls her into the balcony door with such force the glass cracks. She falls to the floor, whimpering. With great effort, he walks over to where she lies. His naked body towering over her, he hammers his fists on the glass door sending broken shards all over both of them.

His anger fuels his strength, further negating the drug's effects. He picks up her broken body, tearing the mesh of the screen door as he carries her through it. He tosses her off the balcony, watching her fall twenty-four floors. He didn't plan it, but she conveniently lands on the roof of his car parked on the street below.

His naked body is bleeding from the shattered glass. He walks over more of the glass slivers, towards his pants, feeling no pain, his feet leaving blood spots on the carpet. He senses the paralytic beginning to work again, falls to his knees and crawls over to reach into his pants pocket.

He pulls out his keyring, enters a self-destruct code, presses the trigger button and blows his entire estate to hell, along with whoever and whatever is in it. His car parked below on the street automatically suffers the same fate.

The paralytic will soon shut down his vital organs and once it reaches his brain, he will be dead. He cannot be found like this. Thinking is difficult, his mind clouding. He needs to act quickly. Before his fingers freeze, he enters a second code and waits. The sacs of poison placed inside his body long ago, for just such a situation, respond to the command. They both open and leak into his bloodstream, one a catalyst, the other an extremely volatile combustible fluid. Once the two are fully combined, his body erupts into flames consuming flesh and bone, leaving only dust behind. His last thought, before the end, *"Goddamn woman!"*

A dark force revels. A Guardian saddened. Nothing to mourn.
A thread aflame.

Rebecca – Curable

Buried amid the multi, omni and ultraversal aspects of The All, hidden in a universe almost forgotten, in a galaxy barely remembered, within a planetary system lost to memory, on the outermost planet, easily mistaken for a moon, a unique story begins to unfold.

It happens on a night that no one at the hospital will ever forget. A barefoot little blond girl with wavy, blond hair and a wonderful smile, estimated to be between three and four years old at the time, appears in the hospital emergency room. She shows up all by herself, on a busy night when the ER staff are preoccupied dealing with multiple injuries from an accident that occurred about two hours earlier.

It is only when all the triaging is done and victims are sent to the appropriate parts of the hospital most suited to their care, that an ER nurse sees the little girl patiently sitting alone in one of the waiting room chairs, looking at a picture book. Assuming she is one of the accident victims or a child of one of the parents, she approaches the girl to inquire. Before she can ask her question, the little girl turns white and falls from the chair, collapsing on the floor.

The ER staff, despite the fatigue from the accident, immediately move into action. An IV is quickly put in as vital signs are taken and they move her to an ER exam room. Readings show the girl still alive, but heart rate extremely slow, blood pressure worrisome for one her age and her temperature indicates she is spiking a fever. X-rays, a CT scan and eventually an MRI are ordered. The little girl remains deathly quiet and still through all of this, though lightly breathing.

The team patiently waits for blood work. The results frighten them, causing them to move her immediately to an isolation room in the pediatric intensive care unit. Here in this galaxy hidden behind a multitude of nebulae, within a universe shielded from view by stellar creations of indescribable magnitude, on a planet with relatively advanced medical technology compared to many others, the little girl with the wavy, blond hair lies in the bed, linked to machines designed to regulate and monitor her extremely comprised immune system.

Specialist after specialist are called in from around the globe to review the case and determine the elusive cause that might lead to a cure, though to no avail. The little girl seems to straddle the gulf between life and death yet continues to survive. The medical community says that her still being alive has more to do with her will to live than with their meaningless but hopeful interventions. The best result for now is that she becomes a case study for medical students.

Then one night, just as dawn becomes day, it happens. She does not die, rather she wakes up as her vital signs stabilize and she apparently returns to complete physical health. She is happy, lucid, bright and cheery, all colour returned, her complexion radiant. On this planet they have a different word for it, but it means miracle. They recognize it was not medical technology that provided the cure, nor they can they determine what has.

New tests and scans are run, multiple blood samples taken, labs done, and all show normal. Well, not quite normal. The number of antibodies running through her system and something unique in her bloodstream, never seen before, give the medical teams pause. There is something else there too, though no one, not regular physicians, nor specialists, immunologists nor even scientists from a host of other branches of medicine and sciences are able to determine its source. They all agree on one thing though: its potential.

If only it could somehow be harnessed, replicated and synthesized, the mystery element could possibly cure a host of diseases that have not yet been eliminated from the population. Explaining to the little girl what they think, what they hope to do and how they would do it, they ask if she will agree to help them. She simply smiles and nods giving a quiet affirmative, "Yes," in a whisper.

The little girl is moved to a secure research facility within the hospital grounds, many levels below the surface, created as quickly as could be, for just this purpose. They do not wish to take any chances with those who might become aware of the situation and seek to remove the little girl and use her for their own less-noble purposes.

Over time, as the little blond girl with the wavy hair continues to grow older, many diseases are cured through the work that is done. Not every disease is eliminated, there is still the common cold, a nasty flu bug, the occasional deadly virus or pandemic. Though even pandemics are minimized, as cures for such things are created much more rapidly using the little girl's immune system and the mystery element's assistance. As the microbiologists, immunologists and other experts warn everyone, diseases always seek to adapt to their environment, finding new ways of thwarting antibodies and immunities by mutating themselves into variants. It is a never-ending battle; constant research and vigilance is required and no one should think the battle against disease will ever be over.

However, even taking into consideration that truth, to say the longevity of the planet's population significantly improved is an understatement. The race prospered, thrived and grew, beginning to reach out beyond their own planet to the stars. They realized they needed to expand to other inhabitable worlds before over-population stretched their own planet's resources beyond capacity. An unfortunate, though not unforeseen by-product of the population's longevity. Most don't even know the source of this mixed blessing and possible curse.

The staff are concerned at times about the little girl's potential loneliness and the absence of parents. No one ever stepped forward to claim her or inquire about her since that fateful night she first appeared. On the other hand, the girl seems to grow in knowledge even without a professional teacher's assistance. She is articulate, polite, able to carry on a conversation with the smartest of the scientific community.

Her laugh is inspiring, her smile intoxicating and she asks questions if she does not understand something, though sometimes it is hard to tell if she is pretending, because she thinks the other person is the one with the wrong answer. She bursts forth in her delightful laugh, shaking her head as though she just discovered something brand new or simply found the other person's idea ludicrous and is trying to be kind.

She can never answer questions about her parents; she seems to think the concept odd and explains she doesn't have any she knows of. When asked if she is lonely, she speaks of all the people that come and go to her room, and how kind they all are to provide her with such good company. She assures them she is fine and particularly enjoys the funnily-dressed older man and the very fashionably-dressed young woman who come to her room sometimes at night to read to her.

The staff shake their heads, thinking the girl must be dreaming it. She mentions it frequently enough though that the more careful personnel grow suspicious and ensure the security cameras around, about and within her room are always functioning properly. Security monitors 24/7 and swears they never see anyone. They do some playbacks for the teams, showing in the middle of the night sometimes the girl is awake and seems to be speaking with someone in the room, but there is no one there. At least not that the cameras show, not even when on infrared. Realizing little children sometimes have imaginary friends, the staff chalks it up to that. After all, the little one has been isolated for so long down in the lower levels, only ever interacting with adults, poked and prodded like a pincushion, always without complaining, making up an imaginary friend or two to talk to seems quite reasonable under the circumstances.

Even the child psychiatrist and child psychologist brought in under the highest levels of security clearances and privacy oaths, agree with the assessment. Imaginary friends are very normal for that age. Considering the circumstances, it is surprising she does not have more issues but none are identified by the experts.

On one particular night, the security team is monitoring the cameras as usual. Staff have bunked down for the night after running some more lab tests to find a cure for a new disease, actually an older disease long thought eliminated, that has mutated and resurfaced. They are close, but not close enough yet to find the cure. They will have to do some more tests with the little girl tomorrow. They all feel great empathy and compassion for her each time they have to run her through that gauntlet over and over, yet the little girl takes it all in stride.

The security cameras go down, an alarm sounds indicating a breach, an unauthorized entry to the level. Security goes into action, weapons drawn and prepared. The four designated staff run to the little girl's room to ensure her safety. Before they even get there, three of them are knocked unconscious by the betrayer from within the group. That one takes off to the little girl's room, his mission to bring her to his accomplices that by now are waiting in a location they previously agreed upon.

They will take the girl from there, eliminating anyone who attempts to stop them, access the roof and the hospital chopper waiting for them, which by now will be under their control. The betrayer is not really that concerned about what will happen to the little girl with the wavy blond hair, he just wants his reward money.

Quite frankly he is sick of her, sick of the work and the money he will receive is more than enough to ease his conscience. He is to go back and lie down with the other four, pretending to also be knocked out. In reality, his accomplices intend to kill him as soon as he passes them the girl, tying up a potential loose end. Unfortunately for this betrayer, he is too greedy to think about that possibility.

The alarm bells wake up the little girl with the blond, wavy hair and she sits up in bed. Unsurprised, she sees the old man dressed in funny clothes who always reads to her. She is excited to have another story read to her. She is surprised to also see the young lady dressed in the prim and proper clothes step out from behind the old man. Her first thought is how nice it will be to have two stories tonight.

The looks on their faces tell her she might not even have one story read to her, let alone two. The figures motion to her to get out of the bed and come to them. She very adeptly removes all the tubes, monitors, wires and the rest of the accoutrements from her body and walks over to them. They both wave their hands in some odd manner and she feels a brisk wind briefly enter the room. A doorway the colour of a rainbow appears. It seems familiar, but she is uncertain why.

Without any hesitation she walks over, clasps a hand from each of them in each of hers and walks with them through the rainbow, leaving the room and the hospital forever. The betrayer enters the room to see only a mix of colours dissipating in the air. The little girl is gone. It happened on a night that none of the staff who knew the little girl with the wavy, blond hair and wonderful smile, will ever forget.

Many staff mourn. The Guardians rejoice. An evil shrieks.

A thread vanishes.

Rez – Neglected

The dream comes again. Rez wakes up in a sweat. It is so odd. In the dream, it always the same; he stands on nothing, looking on from a distance, watching the canvass of the universe. Flaming worlds collide. Stars explode in blinding brilliance. Even space seems to bend around things as he watches galaxies implode, turning in upon themselves and disappear. Always a creeping blackness seeks to cover and submerge everything as the finale to his visionary dream. Then all is gone, only the unsettling quiet of blackness and the absence of life remains. Sometimes it feels like an almost overwhelming outside influence is forcing the dream upon him and that it is not coming from his subconscious creative thought patterns at all.

The sweat pours off his forehead as he sits up and looks over at Kyla and Kitros. His wife and husband lie sleeping quietly, unaware of their partner's turmoil. He does not wish to disturb them. They worked late into the night as it was, readying the nursery for the soon-to-be addition to their family. Well, not that soon, Kyla was only 10 strats along. Their species doesn't achieve full term until the twentieth. They made great progress though. Of course with his disability, he wasn't much help physically, but he could at least give instruction, direction, advice and suggestions. They teased him, referring to him as the "boss man" and asked if they would get fired if they didn't listen. It was all in good fun. Until he fell asleep.

The dreams are so real. Was this the third time? No, fourth within the last three weeks. It is like something or someone familiar is trying to project their thoughts into his mind. He is unable to describe it any other way. Very disturbing. He decides he needs to shake off the remnants of sleep and dreams and prepare for the day. He glances at the time and sees he could easily sneak in a little more rest, but the vividness of the dream has robbed him of that pleasure. He is too much awake. He needs a rinse. He thinks about inviting his partners to join but decides against it. They look so relaxed and they had worked hard last night, they deserve a break.

Still without clothes from his sleeping state, he quietly uses his metal legs and metal arms, shuffling himself to the sitting apparatus that will move him into the rinse station. The water is refreshing at first, then too cold. He shivers during the first rinse cycle until it is completed, and the soap-infused warmer water starts its spray. It isn't too cold or too hot, just perfect. A final rinse, warmer this time and he is ready to begin the day.

By this time, he hears Kyla and Kitros moving in bed. Were they at it again? He laughs. He has no interest in playtime now that he is cleaned up. He makes sure they can hear him, as the apparatus exits the rinse station and moves him towards the storage unit that holds his apparel.

The day promises to be hot and he has already decided he will work outside. Kyla and Kitros are already both on paid leave from their work stations because of the baby. Rez thinks about what manuscript he will work on writing this day. Maybe two or three at once, going back and forth. He needs to sketch some illustrations as well.

Once the disability had manifested, writing, sketching and artwork became Rez's go-to. Fiction, nonfiction, it didn't matter, he possessed a gift for both. His first, an autobiography about living life with his disability, had surprisingly taken off and sold enough copies to provide their family with a hefty on-going profit. Royalties kept flowing in, so he decided to try writing more stories.

The readers, his fans, lapped it up. They couldn't wait for the next publication. Sometimes a series, other times, stand-alones. Always successful, always in demand. He dreads the day when he might have some kind of mental block or writer's funk as he calls it and not be able to produce something as good, or find himself unable to come up with anything at all.

He knows what he is working on for now though: a true log of their family's experience of having a child. From the time they first found out they were having a baby, he planned to make it a diary of love for his fans; a work dedicated to his partners and their new child. It will be a peek into their family's life. He will have to be careful, sensitive, not violate their privacy, or expose too much. He will share just enough to give his readers an understanding of what the journey is like. His publisher loved the idea and encouraged him to proceed, plus, his agent could see dollar signs for everyone.

Some fans are a bit over the top though, he will have to watch that. There are occasionally some who park themselves outside their residence to get a glimpse. They still laugh about the one dedicated fan who tried to scale the fence, not realizing it was electric, got a good shock and then tumbled into their swimming pool. It was a good thing the electricity in their body had dissipated. Kitros, always extremely protective of their union, was angry enough that he picked up the fan and tossed him back over the fence, with a few expletives added for good measure. Rez will be very careful. His parental instincts are already in motion, the drive to protect their child at all costs in place.

He guides his electric chair to the gazebo in their backyard, yelling at the other two, explaining what he is up to. They will continue working on the nursery, while he works outside. Their ever-faithful pet, Dragon, a four-legged canine of mixed breed, joins him outside. Once the animal has done its business on the lawn, it peacefully settles at Rez's feet, occasionally emitting a snore or two, signaling it decided a comfortable nap was in order.

Rez thinks that perhaps he should take a break and write about something different. Perhaps even that dream. Putting it on paper might be cathartic. Maybe give him some insight into what it is all about. He dictates into the computer that transcribes his words into a clean format, auto-correcting along the way. Absentmindedly, he begins sketching some of the visions from his dream as he speaks.

He looks down at his sketch pad, startled to see what he has actually drawn when something covers his eyes. One of his partners fooling around? He shouts with half a laugh at the joke. When he opens his eyes, the world is still black. He can't see. He is blind. He immediately panics wondering if his disability has progressed in some bizarre way. He is scared. Frightened. Thrown off his game. He swears he hears laughter. A crazed fan? He feels Dragon stand up and start barking in an unfriendly tone of warning which quickly turns into a fearful whimper followed by ominous silence.

Even without the barking, Rez recognizes this as something foreign, even alien. Hostile. Nervous. Anxious. Even fearful? Of being discovered? It has something to do with the dream, he knows it. He doesn't know how he knows it, but he does. The word *Devoid* floods his thoughts. Panic-stricken, he tries crawling his way back to the house, yelling for his partners. They can't hear him over the hammering and sawing they are doing in the nursery. His lack of sight causes him to misjudge his location, and he falls into the pool. His metal limbs carry him to the bottom. By the time his partners take a break from working and find him, it is too late.

In this very ancient googolplexian universe, numbered beyond most others, in one of its oldest galaxies, containing an almost-as-old solar system, on the sixth planet from that system's sun, an unborn child loses a father.

A family mourns. The Devoid laughs. A Guardian frustrated.

A thread submersed.

Interlude – Point of Entry

It is frustrated, angry, miserable. It lost track of the little girl. The Devoid understands that she is significant. If only It could find the pathway, It knows, just knows, she can lead It to the goal. There is no trace of her anywhere. How odd that her life thread vibrates differently than all the others It tracks. It vibrates different than any biological or sentient yet encountered. There is something about her, so different it should be obvious, yet The Devoid is unable to detect her unique life thread anywhere.

There must be a hint of an opening, of a gateway somewhere. Its tendrils continue to search the planet and that entire galaxy for any trace of the child, believing the goal to be close. The Nexus, she went to the Nexus. That is the only possible answer. The Gateway must be nearby. The opportunity to swallow it and thus permeate Itself through everywhere is drawing near. It just needs to find the opening the little girl entered.

The Devoid cannot tolerate this loss. Not when so close to the end game. So, It does the unthinkable, It doesn't care anymore anyway. The enemy has already discovered It. There is no need for subtlety any longer, no need to remain hidden. It is so furious at this loss it no longer matters.

The Devoid brings the bulk of Itself to where the girl disappeared, swallowing anything encountered along the way for sustenance. Devouring any obstacles in Its blackness. It anticipates a battle ahead, so acquiring all the energy It can is necessary. Even giving Its presence away is inconsequential. All that matters is finding the opening to the Nexus the girl had undoubtedly used.

It leaves some of Itself scattered throughout, still connected, to sense any other warnings or even other portals to quickly access, force or hold open if the need should arise. Though currently, It is convinced It travels the correct path. It won't be long now until success, It just needs to be patient, thorough. Continue, carefully searching for something that will give way and reveal the point of entry, allowing It to slip through. Then The Devoid will have dominion over everything and everywhere.

Nourishment. Forever.

The barefoot little girl with the wavy blond hair and wonderful smile knows she is getting closer to the very important someone she is going to meet. She starts walking just a bit faster.

PART II

Melody

A melody is a collection of musical tones that are grouped together as a single entity. Most compositions consist of multiple melodies working in conjunction with one another.

A melody, also tune, voice, or line, is a linear succession of musical tones that the listener perceives as a single entity. In its most literal sense, a melody is a combination of pitch and rhythm.

CHAPTER ONE

Duet #1

A duet is a musical composition for two performers in which the performers have equal importance to the piece.

Lindsay floats in space, uncertain if she is still alive or has been dead for a while. Everything seems off. She hears noises though, voices, loud, yelling, screaming, perhaps even explosions. It is not that long ago she remembers, or thinks she remembers, hearing people bending over her, talking about her condition. Maybe medical people, trying to decide whether she would live or not, wondering about pulling out life support. That's it. They thought she was hopeless, so removed everything that was keeping her alive. Apparently, she still has a pulse and can breathe on her own. She vaguely remembers their surprised comments at that. Then everything changed.

It is coming back to her now. Explosions started up again. People yelled as debris fell from everywhere. The medical people screamed at one another, some fell over bleeding, others scrambled to move people out of beds. This wasn't a hospital though, more like a makeshift rescue thing in the middle of the street. Not much else comes back to her.

She feels a thump, like she has just re-entered her body after falling a long way.

She tries to sit up and manages successfully to do so. Only a little dizzy, she takes a few breaths, while looking at the devastation surrounding her. She needs to get away. She isn't sure to where, but she remembers the falling debris, the screaming, sees some bloodied bodies lying around her and decides she needs to do whatever it takes to find a safer refuge.

The acrid smell of things burning assaults her nostrils. Lindsay takes a few deep breaths and realizes even the air tastes foul. She still isn't even sure what occurred. A war? Just her city? Maybe the whole country is under attack? She looks up for the first time and gasps. The sky looks like it is on fire, a brazen red, mixed with black smoke permeating everything overhead. She thinks of wildfires and their smoky effect that can travel for miles. This is much worse and brings tears to her eyes, whether from the seeing the sky on fire, or her surroundings on the ground, she cannot tell.

She pushes the thoughts away, resisting, avoiding any thinking that might make her panic. She needs to concentrate on getting off the bed and putting one foot in front of the other. A step at a time. That sounds ironically humorous in her mind and she smiles. Gingerly, she tests the ground to see if she can maintain her balance. Wonderful! That works. Lindsay starts walking slowly but something pulls at her, holding her back. She feels a pain in her arm and upon examining the source, recognizes an IV line is still attached to her.

She winces as she removes it, and looking down realizes she is wearing only a blue hospital gown. She sees her arms and legs are covered in bruises, some swollen and a nasty shade of black. She notices strips of cloth fastened over what she assumes are some of her worst injuries. Maybe there are stitches, but she doesn't feel like checking. She isn't bleeding, at least not anywhere she can see.

Lindsay pauses and looks up to see portions of buildings which have crumbled, others sway, waiting to fall, roads are cracked and bodies lie in random places. She can't tell if those people are only injured or if most are already dead, although moaning and distant cries provide some clue. She has an idea and walks towards a couple of the bodies that are not too far. She doesn't think she is ready to run yet, but walking fast is a start. She has never seen a dead body before other than during funerals with open caskets. Those bodies were all prettied up, with make up and dressed nicely, so different than what confronts her now.

The first, a man, is pale, bloody with pieces of sharp metal sticking out of his forehead, crumpled in an abnormal position as though captured in free fall and smashed to the ground. He looks terrible but even worse is the smell. The aroma of death fills the area and her sense of smell is under attack again. She feels the bile in her throat rise and fill her mouth.

She forces herself to swallow so she can focus on her original intent. She is looking to see if there is a cell phone nearby.

She needs to call her parents. Let them know she is alive and, even though the thought brings tears to her eyes, find out if they are alive too. No luck. Lindsay doesn't see anything near the man, and although she detests the idea, she searches his pockets too. The only thing she finds is a key card which she pays little attention to, it is not what she is looking for, so she tosses it on the ground. There is nothing. Then she realizes the corpse is dressed in pyjamas rather than clothes. Something clicks, and she runs to where the key card landed. She examines it once more, recognizes the symbol and goes back to the body.

She hasn't had the courage or the desire to turn it over and see his face, but now she feels compelled to do so. It is one of her neighbours from two floors below her. A nice retired gentleman, always polite, always willing to lend a hand if she needed help carrying groceries up to her apartment. Lindsay stifles a scream, moans and cries a bit. He has probably been dead from the time she started falling. This is too much, but she still desperately needs to find a phone.

She moves on a bit farther down the sidewalk. The burning smells, the odour of death, the moaning she hears from farther away are becoming too much for her to take in. For the moment she ignores it all and focuses on the task at hand. She approaches the next corpse.

It's actually two corpses. The sight is unseemly and heartbreaking. A child of probably seven or eight, dead in its mother's arms. She was obviously holding the child close to her, perhaps to protect it from falling debris, but there is no way to tell. Lindsay does not see any obvious wounds, but there are burn marks on both of them. Sores and lesions, their skin peeling in some places, along with pockmarks.

The thought, *"Oh my god, radiation burns,"* enters her mind and she is terrified. She searches frantically for any sign of a phone; she doesn't care if looking in a purse or pockets is invasive or not, she must find a phone and she does. She prays there is no pass code and manages to turn it on. She starts dialing until she realizes there is no symbol for a signal. The phone must have broken during whatever happened.

Lindsay keeps going and every time she comes across a dead body, she puts aside her fears and the disgusting smells, searching bodies, pockets, purses, backpacks, knapsacks, even kids' lunch boxes, whatever might hold a phone. She does find two or three more but all the same result; none have signals. She concludes cell towers have been knocked out or destroyed. To confirm her assumptions, she hears a rumbling, perhaps an echo of an explosion, followed by an ominous darkness. Any limited lighting left around her, whether streetlights, or in the few buildings still standing, or random other places, is all extinguished.

Night is coming in a city gone dark with death and destruction. Lindsay can't help but think of movies about zombies and alien invasions and questions if they have become real. An unearthly crashing noise shakes her surroundings and she looks up to see a thirty-storey building about ten blocks from her crash to the ground, the vibrations shaking everything. She wishes it would have just fallen on her and ended this hell she has found herself in.

There is no way to communicate with her parents or to find out if they even still exist. She sits down on the cement, surrounded by the last five corpses she searched, and sobs uncontrollably for a long time. By the end of it she is both cursing God and asking for his help and begging him to answer, *"Why?"*

God lives up to her expectations and says nothing.

Where to now? She can't stay here, especially if she is close to whatever might be giving off more radiation. Lindsay thinks to herself, *"Apparently I still have some survival instincts.*" With no sense of direction, she starts walking away from what is left of the dead who surround her. She is now many blocks away from the makeshift hospital where she woke up. At least it saved her life. Maybe. For what though?

She continues paying more attention to the devastation above and around her, rather than to where her feet are stepping. She feels a cool wetness when her left foot steps into a puddle the size of a small pond that has inexplicably formed on the sidewalk and on part of the damaged road before her.

There are vehicle wrecks all over the roads and walkways and signs of accidents where drivers must have run into each other in their panic to escape. Lindsay notices three transports twisted into the oddest positions as though a giant hand had picked them up, crushed them and then kept ramming them into the ground repeatedly just for some sadistic pleasure. She looks past the wreckage scenes, scanning for burst pipes or some source that would have caused the puddle, but sees nothing. Not unexpectedly though. It is growing darker and there is very little that is making sense anyway.

The cold water on her foot feels refreshing so she puts the other one in as well. She isn't sure how deep the thing goes, so she carefully takes a few more steps forward, taking time to feel the cold water's embrace. She walks into the puddle further until the water is up to her knees. It almost feels healing which is odd. There is a warmth to it now as well. She concludes the heat may be due to the unseen source. Lindsay hesitates for a moment worrying about fallen electrical wires that might be lingering around close to the water. How ironic would that be, to wake up alive after being left for dead and then get electrocuted by her own carelessness.

She decides to venture in a little further, after all the puddle can't be that deep. Bad idea. A mistake. Without warning, she is falling deep into the pond. It is now over her head and she keeps sinking. She struggles to swim upwards, but her body is far too weak for that fight. She realizes she will not die of electrocution but drowning instead. She wonders if people cry under water as they drown.

Something is not right though. She is still descending, but the water is getting even warmer and she swears she can still breathe. This is strange. If she is as deep as she believes, her lungs should be filled with water by now, but they are not. The whole thing is making her sick to her stomach but at the same time, the water's effect seems to be healing all her aches and pains. She feels more alive than she has been in days, well, maybe ever. How can that be when she is drowning?

The falling motion stops and things reverse. Totally surprised, Lindsay feels herself rising. She is moving upwards, back to the surface. This is a good thing, though she does not relish the thought of being back in the middle of all the chaos, explosions, screaming and death. She is sick of the smells and thinks to herself, *"I swear I will throw up on the next corpse. I can't handle this anymore."*

She closes her eyes and steels herself to face what is coming. She feels a tug or maybe more of a strong pull, lifting her out of the puddle. Her eyes still closed, she feels herself pop out of the water as if thrown, and landing on something soft. It feels like grass. How can that be? Is there somehow another exit to the puddle, to a park that was at least partially undamaged? She expected to find herself back on the cement sidewalk and roadway that surrounded the pond.

Shaken, Lindsay opens her eyes verifying that it is grass under her bare feet. She looks around and sees the pool she just emerged from or at least thinks it must be the one, because there are still a few ripples. She takes in a deep breath, tries smelling her surroundings and realizes there is no aroma of death and certainly no evidence of destruction anywhere.

Amazed, she looks around and sees only other pools. So many, as far as she can see in the distance and probably more beyond that. They all seem peaceful and without motion. She shakes her head in disbelief, confusion and wonder, thinking, *"This is incredible and nonsensical. Did God really answer my prayer?"* She decides to test that theory.

"Am I dead?" she calls aloud.

The responder makes her scream. Loud and long.

*   *   *

Bran is sinking, his protective clothing starting to ripple and catch fire from the intense heat of the boiling water surrounding him. He does not have the energy or wherewithal to even try to swim upwards. There is no point; by the time he would reach the surface, his body would be nothing but a charred husk anyway. He has seen that happen to others before. Better to let the waters claim him than put his family through seeing him that way.

He switches his thoughts from that grisly musing and focusses on the blackness he had seen eclipsing his world's sun just before he was sent tumbling off his craft by the collision. What was that anyway? He thinks it didn't seem natural. It was concerning. He hopes his island is okay, his friends, even his world. Bran says a silent prayer as the heat continues to rip away at his gear which is now starting to shrivel. It won't be long before his skin feels it too.

His thoughts turn to his sister. He will finally be with her, see her again. This is consoling. It will not protect him from the intense pain of the burning flames about to rip into his body, but it is something at least. After the agony will come peace and his sister. Those are both good things.

He doesn't know how much time he has left or why he suddenly feels himself dropping deeper towards the bottom of the boiling sea. In fact, it is more like he is simultaneously being pushed down from up above while being dragged down deeper by something below. Bran has never heard of this before but then again, no one who had fallen into the flaming sea ever survived to tell any tales of their experience. Perhaps this is what death is like down here, and he is just feeling the sensations of the end to his physical body.

He realizes he is still breathing, which is odd. The breathing apparatus that holds his methane should have stopped working by now. He chances a look down and is surprised to see the water he approaches bubbling furiously. A closer look informs him it is seething around something. That something is exactly where he is being pushed and pulled down towards. He cannot tell what it is until he is much closer. Unbelieving, he sees a calm surface within the sea. Is that a small pool? How is that possible? Even more confusing, it is not bubbling, but remains perfectly calm and still, in the centre of the angry churning waters circling it.

Maybe this is simply the route to his end and to the place where he will finally be reunited with his sister. He closes his eyes anticipating both the worst and the best. A transformation of life into death and maybe into life again of a different sort. That is what his faith informs him. In his mind he thinks another prayer to the Powers, thanking them for his life, asking that his death not be too painful and praising them that he will be reunited with loved ones again.

Still feeling the push from above and a pull from below, he passes through the pond at the bottom of the boiling sea. Without warning, he feels himself ejected from the pond, his eyes open, his gear, though somewhat shrivelled, still on, including his protective helmet. He lands on the ground and looks around, sitting in awe and disbelief.

Bran sees a line of pools like the one he just surfaced from. They go on as far as his eyes can see. He is sitting on grass, near a grove of majestic trees that also go on forever, their treeline continuing far off into the distance. The trees are incredibly tall, stretching upwards into a clear crisp blue sky, so much so he cannot see their tops. Even his seven-foot stature, typical for his race and age, is dwarfed by the trees' incredible height.

The trees are unfamiliar, their shapes unique, but all bear leaves lush with a variety of radiant colours, many of which he has never seen in his life. These impossibly tall trees form a hedge around the innumerable pools, apparently acting as a barrier of some sort. His island home grows trees, here and there, but there is nothing remotely recognizable in the sight before him.

If this is his final resting place, it is very odd because there is no one else present. Not his sister, nor friends or family lost before him. This is very different from what he was expecting. Perhaps he isn't dead after all.

Maybe he crossed through some magical doorway that saved him. Maybe the Powers are behind it. After all, he had prayed, although this is not the answer he expected. Maybe the Powers have something else in mind. Maybe they are responsible for the pushing and pulling he felt that drew him deep into the water and brought him to this place. Maybe he lives because he still has a purpose. Maybe he could even breathe here if he took off his helmet. Too many maybes, but the last one intrigues him.

Bran begins to undo the locks in his helmet preparing to remove it, when another pool starts to make a noise and he turns to see ripples forming across it. He is curious, anticipating that something is going to happen but uncertain what that might be. The ripples grow in intensity, now becoming small waves disturbing the original peacefulness of the water. Bran watches in amazement as a figure bounds out of the water as though being thrown and lands on the grass a bit of distance from where he sits. Bran notices the figure is smaller in height than him and wears only a single garment. He concludes by its shape it is probably a kind of female creature. His people do not yet have the vocabulary to distinguish other species, or even refer to them as humanoids. For a brief moment, he hopes it might be his sister sent to welcome him. He quickly realizes he is wrong and sets that hope aside. He wonders if he will be able to communicate with the stranger, if he will understand her or she him, or if they even speak the same language. His question is answered when, astonished, he hears her exclaim, "Am I dead?"

Trying to reassure her, Bran answers, "No, I don't think so. I don't think we are."

The creature, which he now observes is much shorter than he, turns towards the sound of his voice and begins screaming. She screams loudly and for a long time. Bran is dismayed. He doesn't know if this is part of her language, and if so, he doesn't understand a word. Or perhaps he somehow frightened her. Bran realizes he is still wearing his helmet and his damaged protective gear. He wonders if she is not familiar with that, and guesses his appearance shocked her.

While still looking at her, and saying, "I'm sorry if I frightened you," he slowly and deliberately removes his black protective helmet, and then what remains of his shiny red outerwear. Some of it falls apart in his hands, a result of the boiling sea's flames, while other parts stick to his inner clothing and when he pulls on it some of the inner pieces end up tearing as well. He does his best and when done, he still wears most of his grey and blue inner garments though some parts are quite well shredded, with holes here and there.

His people don't have much hesitation in terms of being nude around each other. He knew the other peoples that they met on their journeys among the closer islands had varying levels of comfort with that, so he wishes to be cautious as he has no idea what this creature's customs might be. He isn't even sure she is intelligent, but he doesn't wish to offend or upset her further.

He notices the female creature wears only a very loose-fitting blue gown, with bare arms and bare feet. Bran can't tell for sure, but there don't seem to be any other clothes beneath the gown so perhaps that is the custom of her people, wherever she is from. Her long auburn hair appears dishevelled and he also observes some bruising on her arms and legs. He wonders if that had been caused by her landing when she was ejected from the pool.

Now that his helmet is removed, he looks directly at her, doing his best to smile, despite being just as confused and perhaps as scared as her, he repeats, "I am so sorry to have frightened you. I have removed my protective gear, so maybe this is better?"

The creature stopped screaming when Bran started removing his helmet and now watches him anxiously. She shakes her head up and down, perhaps attempting to form some words but having a hard time doing so. She looks Bran over slowly, fearfully, finally blurting out as though not knowing what else to say, "Why are you so tall?" taking in his seven-foot athletic frame.

Somewhat stunned by the unexpected question, Bran responds, "Well, I'm the average height for my people. Some of my elders are much taller."

The stranger stands to her feet, her eyes focused on his head, "Well, what's wrong with your hair?"

"Wrong?" Bran is stupefied by the question and begins to think the creature is either somewhat out of sorts or perhaps its journey has caused it to lose its mind. He puts his hand through his hair and reaches behind his head to verify everything is still in place. "I don't understand what you mean. My hair seems fine."

"Yes, wrong! Blue and orange don't go together. Certainly not in a ponytail! At least you have a nice tan!"

As though she simply just ran out of energy, she sits back down on the grass.

Regaining some composure, she looks back up at Bran apologetically,

"I'm so sorry. Those were such random questions. Dumb ones really. Maybe insulting, which I didn't mean to be. What I really want to ask is, 'Where am I? Why have you brought me here?'"

She stares directly at him this time, surprised by his well-chiselled facial features, strong jawline and exceptionally bright, though slightly slanted, bluish-green eyes. The shape of the stranger's eyes reminded her of people she knew but seemed unable to specifically remember who or from where.

Bran, amazed at how easily he understands her, wonders how she knows his language. "I have the same questions. I didn't bring you here, but I did see you arrive. I don't know where we are, or why we are here. I also don't know how you understand and can speak my language? Which island are you from?"

Startled by the young tone of the stranger's voice, she cautiously begins, "My name is Lindsay. But give me a minute. This is all very confusing and I just got out of the hospital. Well sort of a hospital, I don't know. I think my world was falling apart, like maybe a war. Then I stepped into a puddle. I'm not from an island, well, I mean not the way you might think. Though the city I lived in was sometimes called the island of… the island of… well that's strange, I can't remember the name of it. Maybe I got a concussion when I fell. I don't know how or where I fell, I know I did though. I don't suppose it's important anymore. Well, it feels less important. Then, like I said, I stepped into a puddle. I thought I was drowning for a bit, and then here I am. Wherever here is. Then you scared me."

"Again, sorry about that. My name is Bran. I am from… from… well, that's odd, I don't remember the name either. I do remember I was in a race on the boiling sea."

Bran looked directly into the stranger's bright blue eyes as he spoke, not an eye colour of any of his people. He was about to comment on that when Lindsay interrupted.

"Like a boat race? What do you mean by boiling sea? I don't think we have those where I'm from. Or not that I remember. Island explains your tan though. Sorry, go on."

Bran continues his story, explaining how he was knocked off his racing vessel into the boiling sea and found himself submerged, assuming he was going to burn to death until a pool appeared in at the bottom of the boiling waters. He described how he felt himself both pushed and pulled through it until he found himself here, sitting on the grass. He explains to her that it was only a short time after his arrival that she appeared, thrown out of a different pool and landing not far away from him.

He makes one more observation, "I may have no idea where we are, but I must say the methane here is excellent. I was afraid I wouldn't be able to breathe if I took my helmet off. It was out of breathable methane anyway. Quite a coincidence. Very fortunate we landed in a place like this."

Lindsay confused, interrupts, "But I can breathe here too, and I breathe oxygen, not methane. I don't know what it's like to be a methane breather, but I am definitely not one. O2 for me. We are obviously not even the same species."

"Yet we can understand each other and both still breathe here. What a wondrous place!" Bran exclaims, and then with even more excitement points out, "Look! I saw bruises and cuts on your arms and legs when you first arrived. They are gone now. Vanished like you have been healed. By the Powers, this is miraculous!"

Lindsay examines herself, checking to verify Bran's words. Her wounds are indeed healed, and even the cloths that had covered the more serious wounds have vanished.

Bran nods his head as she confirms her healing, "Yes, this is amazing! It's so quiet and peaceful here. Have you noticed there are no sounds whatsoever? No birds, no breeze, nothing. It's almost like time is standing completely still."

Lindsay now takes a moment to look at her surroundings. She is stunned at the innumerable pools and the grand forest that surrounds them. She is somewhat overwhelmed by the magnificence that fills her sight. *"There's not even a sun in the sky, yet it's so bright! I wonder..."* Smiling, she turns and questions Bran with her guess, "Are you sure this isn't heaven, and you are an angel?"

"I am definitely not that," responds Bran quickly. The word *"angel"* may not translate properly into his language, yet he understands what she means.

"I see," Lindsay's tone of voice expresses disappointment. Hesitantly, she tries another question, "Or are you sure, I mean, are you certain," she pauses and restarts, "Are you sure we are not both dead?"

"No, not at all!"

Lindsay and Bran, with startled looks, stare at each other, realizing neither of them has said anything.

"Did you...?" Bran gestures, looking around, but sees no one else.

"Yes, I did, though I could not tell if it was only in my mind or also aloud," Lindsay confirms.

"Yes, same here. What do we do? Do we answer it?" Bran is cautious but does not sense danger.

Lindsay is beginning to feel less nervous and frightened than when she first arrived. At the very least, she is curious about the stranger she has just met. "I don't know, I was kind of enjoying listening to your story of how you arrived."

"Same here," Bran says, expressing his own desire to learn more from this odd creature.

Lindsay is growing more confident, "What if we just ignore whatever said that, and get to know each other. Like learn about each other. I mean more than just how we came to be here. But about our lives. Your island

and your races."

"Yes, and your island of a city whose name you can't remember and what you did there. My people love to share stories. Would you like to start, or shall I?"

"Excellent!" The Voice from nowhere speaks again. "Yes, tell each other your stories. It's a very important thing to do. Very important indeed."

The two look around again. Seeing nothing, they agree to ignore whoever or whatever that was and oddly enough, the idea of paying no attention to it did not seem peculiar at all to them. They don't feel anything threatening from the speaker. Rather, the Voice is calming, casting away doubts and fears. Even though, for some reason, they aren't that interested in learning more about it, just about each other.

Bran tells Lindsay everything he can remember from his sister's death to his mourning, his races and so much more. When he is done, Lindsay takes her turn and shares what she remembers, from growing up as a little girl and into adulthood, including all the decisions that led her to the belief that she is to do something very significant with her life. Just as her parents taught her, she was determined to make a positive difference in her corner of the universe. Neither one of them can remember the names of the places they came from. By the time they are done talking, they forget that it mattered.

A Guardian smiles. The Nexus breathes. Two threads join.
The Devoid oblivious.

CHAPTER TWO

Duet #2

A duet is a musical composition for two performers in which the performers have equal importance to the piece.

Tavarez wakes with a start. Momentarily forgetting his dilemma, he tries to walk on solid ground. No such luck. It all comes back to him. Still dressed in his brightly coloured climbing gear, he hangs in mid-air, stuck between two jagged cliffs. *"What a stupid idea this was in the first place,"* he chastises himself. He is helpless. Suspended in limbo. Nothing to grab on to. He will likely starve to death hanging like this.

"At least it isn't windy. What a dumb thought." The wind is picking up. It starts swinging

him a little at a time. If it grows any stronger, he is doomed. Tavarez understands he does not have the knowledge, skills or experience to know what to do or even attempt something risky that might save him. He is stuck. He can not even call out for help with his mind; he is useless at that too.

The wind grows stronger, moving his hapless unsteady form back and forth, but not too close to the jagged rocks on either side of him. He just wanted some alone time to process, to think. How much more solitary can one get? To die totally alone out here in what always appears as beautiful scenery at a distance. Alone.

Suddenly he becomes aware he is not alone, at least not mentally. A force rips into his mind, breaking down every insecurity, every artificial protective barrier Tavarez had unconsciously set up as a child. He has a glimpse of his childhood and a stranger trying to gain entrance to his mind in a bad way, an abusive, evil, unwanted way. He unexpectedly remembers how he had used all his childhood pre-formed mental energy to block that. He had succeeded. But now he recognizes what actually happened and what the cost has been.

He doesn't have time to think about it too long though; the force sweeping into his mind is substantial and he cannot block it. Not like when his auto-defences protected him as a child, there is no preventing this intrusion. His mind surges with images of a darkness, of a *Devoid*, something hungry and quite ravenous, determined to swallow whole universes.

What in the name of all the Denizens is happening? Tavarez tries to calm himself and listen. This becomes more difficult as the wind grows fiercer and his swinging brings him closer than he wishes to possible death. He needs to listen though. Figure out what is happening both to him and whoever is broadcasting this message. They are an extremely strong telepath, whoever they are. He also senses they are not being malicious. They are trying to be helpful, maybe even a cry for help on their part. At the very least, they are providing a warning of impending danger. Serious, deadly danger. Tavarez picks that much up.

The images continue, filling his mindscape with things unimaginable. Tavarez relaxes, lets it all in and then ventures to broadcast a question out. He is surprised at how easily he can do that now. It is as though the stranger who invaded his mind space also provided him with the skills and knowledge to do everything he always thought he would never be able to do.

He hears the voices, sees the visions, understands. This is a different Tavarez from another universe. Unbelievable! But the other opens his mind to Tavarez as well. It is all true, the being is a genius. Tavarez incorporates what he can absorb into his own mind, owning the other's knowledge and experiences. He learns quickly: *"The Devoid is coming."*

Images of danger, death, destruction and the name -*The Devoid*-overwhelm him. The mocking voice he heard earlier that had no visible or apparent source. *"Was that it?"* He sees tendrils in his mind, visions of them from his counterpart. And something more. In the background of the other's mind, he can see The Devoid discharge tendrils outwards to other locations. It discreetly followed the other Tavarez's warning message as it was broadcast out across universes. It tracked all the locations where the message went. Is it chasing the variations of Tavarez or just some? This is too much to grasp.

His mind is now reeling. He tries to reach out to the other Tavarez again but this time senses something awful, he senses the other's intent. He is going to sacrifice himself to save his world, his entire universe perhaps. Tavarez knows how the other is going to do it. He cries, *"No!"* into the other's mind and receives only a desperate, *"No other way,"* response. The other flashes him an instruction of how to cut the connection between them lest this Tavarez suffer the same fate.

Three things happen simultaneously: Tavarez cuts the connection, the storm of which the wind had only been a harbinger moves in with dark clouds of fury, rain, thunder and lightning, the entirety of it focused on Tavarez. The wind begins whipping him about mercilessly like a rag doll about to be cut into pieces by jagged rocks that have now become knives of death. Lightning crackles all around him, as thunder rolls. Tavarez, now a target, waits for the final strike.

He observes something else in the dark clouds; this is no mere coincidence. He recognizes the blackness, the form from the other's mind projections. This is part of the all-consuming Devoid. He has no idea why It targets him in particular. Awareness grows and he understands, at least partially. The other version of himself from however many universes away saved his people by his sacrifice. He also warned Tavarez. Could Tavarez save his people too? He must try.

He feels the power of the other version of himself churning within him. If he channels it, he could do the same thing the other Tavarez did. At least for his world. One mind blast sharing the same images of danger, death and destruction, warning everyone of the Devoid, maybe they could all do something together. Unlike the other Tavarez's world, the people of his world were all telepaths. That might be their salvation. Even if he does not survive, at least he will have warned his people and given them a chance.

He looks up. The darkness grows deeper, the storm more furious. The Devoid is coming for him. Not just him, likely his entire world. He takes a deep breath, looks deeply inside himself, focusses even in the midst of everything else trying to destroy him and lets everything he has learned, seen, felt, and heard, all that he appropriated in milliseconds into his mind flow out to everyone on his world. In this singular moment, Tavarez is the strongest mind on his planet.

He closes his eyes, exhausted. He has no energy left to fight what is coming for him. No energy to fight The Devoid. Perhaps he has saved his world though. Another voice breaks in. The same disturbing one from before.

"You failed. You first, then your world. I will feed and leave nothing."

Tavarez attempts to push it away but it's a futile effort. He is too exhausted from the mind blast he sent throughout his planet and does not possess the stamina to exercise more of his recovered ability.

Wait. He hears something. Something is changing. The darkness that has been approaching is hesitating, moving much more slowly. Did it work? Was the thing lying to him? A tease to make him give up? Was he hearing his people in his mind? The lightning is getting

closer. This is it. Maybe he saved all the others, but there is no way of saving himself.

*   *   *

Matos Jason tumbles inside the strange vortex that captured him just as he watched his galaxy vanish into blackness. Overwhelmed with what he witnessed, he is having difficulty gaining his balance which is extremely odd, considering his capability of flight. He wonders if perhaps gravity, or even all the normal laws of physics do not work within his current prison.

"What is he in anyway? A ship? A black hole?" When the vortex first captured him, he asked himself, *"Is this the opening of one end of a wormhole, if so, is it a natural or a constructed one, and if constructed, by what advanced race?"* Now his enhanced senses tell him something feels different, *"Wait! Is it slowing down? Yes it is!"*

As it slows, Matos Jason feels the shift in velocity and regains his balance. He is able to stand and sort of fly, at least in a steady, non-tumbling way. He thinks again of the blackness he saw consuming everything, frustration and anger rising within. He feels so helpless. The one who wanted to do nothing but help others his entire life. Save people. He had saved nothing. It was all gone.

He has no time to dwell on this further for abruptly another mind breaks into his. He is not certain of the source but the image in his mindscape is a picture of the same blackness he had seen just before he was pulled into the wormhole if that's indeed what it is. He needs to find the source, find the person projecting this and see what they know.

Jason knows about telepaths, has even worked with some, but is not one himself. Most were guarded, respectful and cautious how they used their powers unlike whoever is currently broadcasting this message. A message fraught with both urgency and panic, as well as fear. The fear of death fast approaching is evident and tangible.

Matos Jason wonders if there is a way of steering the mysterious thing he is inside of. He tests each corner of the vessel, he does not know what it else to call it, to see if the telepathic message is stronger in one direction than another. It is. He positions himself against that side of the vessel and pushes it in that direction, as though he were flying, using all his strength to steer it. He is in fact piloting the wormhole ship, as he now names it.

With no clue what to do when he reaches the source of the mind projection, he continues pushing forward, veering accordingly to ensure the thing stays on course, determined by whatever direction the frequency is the strongest. Another image fills his mind as he manoeuvres. The picture of a young man suspended on ropes hanging in mid-air between mountainous cliffs boasting sharp deadly rocks on either side. The young man sways in the wind, the centrepiece of a dark storm. A heavy downpour and lightning strikes flash around him, not yet hitting him, but getting much too close. Intuitively, Matos Jason understands the young man is the source of the telepathic message.

Matos Jason also sees the darkness is much more than a storm. There is something uncomfortably and hauntingly familiar about it. He now knows its name from the young man's mind blast: *The Devoid*. He hates it already. The wormhole ship slows down. Loud noises outside his vessel crackle, boom and echo ferociously. Realizing it is the storm, the same picture he sees in his mind, informs him he must be close to the young man. Tavarez, that is his name. Imprinted along with the other information. Tavarez.

Maybe he can save this one at least. The wormhole ship comes to a complete stop. The downpour rages and the whole area is covered in dark clouds, Tavarez is unable to see a thing. Certainly not the ship or Matos Jason's hand when it reaches out. He does hear something though: above the thunder and the wind, an external voice shouts above the storm, "Here, take my hand!"

He opens his eyes trying to see what or who is speaking. He recognizes immediately this is not a voice in his head. With the infusion of information from the other Tavarez, his skills are already developing at an unbelievably fast pace and growing well-honed enough to know the difference between internal and external voices. He hears the words again, "Take my hand! Hurry!"

A golden glove appears in front of him, close enough he can see it clearly. Tavarez does not speak, but conveys the message, *"I am stuck, all twisted up on these ropes,"* and the verbal response comes back, "It's fine. I will deal with those but take my hand first."

Tavarez reaches one hand out into the darkness, feeling a firm strong grip, he grasps back as hard as his tired body will allow, as if his life depends on it. It does. He imagines he sees a thin slice of fire coming towards him, and in seconds he feels the ropes let go. The gloved hand pulls him to safety, as a bolt of lightning strikes the spot where he hung in futile desperation only seconds ago.

Matos Jason sees the darkness surge again. He closes his eyes, not wanting to see a repeat of the same fate occur elsewhere. Tavarez sees something different; he sees the blackness draw back. Something else is pushing it away. He reaches out and feels a billion plus minds aimed at the blackness in a fury of force. Whatever kind of vessel the stranger pulled him into, the door of it shuts just as Tavarez sees the sky clear. As the door to the vessel closes, he hears the unified voices of his planet, *"Thank you Tavarez, wherever you are, you have saved us. You have saved your world. We are sorry. We love you. Thank you."*

The grateful voices are followed by a shrill, hateful scream in his mind, causing him to both tremble in fear and smile in relief. He knows the terrifying shriek came from The Devoid. He also understands it was forced to retreat.

All the voices are gone, there is only silence. Whatever mode of transportation he is in starts moving rapidly, causing both he and the stranger to tumble around each other until everything stops, dead still. They both fall to the floor. Neither have any idea how long the trip lasted. For all they know it could have been for days or only moments. When the thing comes to a complete stop, the exit door re-forms. The vessel moves again in such a way that they are both tossed out into what appears to be the sands of a desert. Before either says anything, the thing that carried them to this place simply vanishes.

Matos Jason and Tavarez look at each other for a few silent moments. Tavarez finally breaks the silence, "Thank you for saving me, whoever you are. My name is…"

"Tavarez, yes, I know, I picked it up from your mind blast. That was intense, boy."

"Yes, I'm so sorry, I am still getting used to it, and most of what you saw, well all of it, came from another me, a different person I mean, sorry it's hard to explain."

"That's okay," retorted Jason, "We can talk about telepathic protocols and pleasantries later. First, we should probably figure out where we are. My name is Matos, Matos Jason."

Matos scans their surroundings while they talk. The desert sands go on forever in all directions. Oddly, though it is bright, there is no sun in the cloudless sky, which appears as endless as the sands. While one might think the desert heat would be stifling, the temperature is quite comfortable. All of this puts Matos Jason on his guard, alert and cautious; he expects an encounter with danger any time. He is about to share his concerns with the young man, but Tavarez speaks first.

"Oh, nice to meet you Matos Jason, and again, thanks for saving me. We saved my whole planet and thanks to you, I survived too."

Now removed from the darkness of the transportation that so unceremoniously dumped them on these desert sands, they can actually see each other in the brightness of their surroundings. Tavarez notes that Matos Jason is slightly taller than he, with thinning black and grey hair that might betray his age as older. It is hard to tell if that is true, as Matos Jason's face does not give away his age. If anything, it only communicates friendliness and an earnest eagerness to help, as do his welcoming but penetrating green eyes, though they are shaped in more of an oval way that is unlike Tavarez's own people.

Except for the golden gloves, his saviour is mostly dressed in black and grey, a tight-fitting suit of body armour, that outlines extremely strong muscles belonging to a very athletic, in-shape individual, one dedicated to physical training. The suit appears to be made of material which Tavarez is certain he has never seen before. Matching black boots stretch up almost to his new acquaintance's knees and end in a fold, locking them in to the suit's pants.

Tavarez realizes he easily could learn more through his unleashed telepathic powers, even if just to ensure he is not in danger. The stranger's earlier comment about telepathic protocols both surprised and reassured him, so he let the idea go for now. He knows he can call upon them if necessary. His assessment is interrupted by Matos Jason's question, "Are you sure your world is safe now? That blackness devoured my home world and solar system, maybe my entire galaxy, if not our whole universe. I only barely escaped when that thing we just got out of appeared and sucked me into it. I saw everything go black and vanish as it captured me. Now that I think about it, maybe capture is not the right word to describe what it did to me. Rescue is better, I think maybe it rescued me."

Matos Jason assesses the young stranger as he speaks. He notes Tavarez is young, shorter than him though not by much and dressed in what might be sports gear of some kind. After all, the youth was in the mountains, and the brown hiking boots are a bit of a giveaway along with the rest of the gear tucked in and hanging from the vest and pants pockets.

The colours of the gear are rather bright, a combination of reds, oranges and greens that should not have matched the brown boots and yet they do. Matos laughs to himself, thinking maybe the young man is a novice and had outfitted himself, or been taken advantage of by whomever sold him such an odd blend of colours and equipment. *"Not important at the moment,"* he reminds himself.

He looks closer and observes that Tavarez's face has natural indents, and an odd-shaped ridge across his nose. The youngster's bright red hair, flecked with streaks of black and white, is cut short, at the sides and back, though a few longer strands fall forward at the front, not quite reaching his eyes. Ears and other body features are similar to what he is familiar with, but the circular-shaped eyes set further back in the young man's face indicate Tavarez is undoubtedly from a race he has never encountered before. Matos Jason decides he is not in any danger, at least not at the moment. In fact, he finds himself drawn to this unique individual, although unable to explain why.

Tavarez's curiosity leads to more questions for his rescuer. "So I notice you are dressed all in black. Well, except for the golden gloves! That's a great colour! Is this normal dress for your people? Honestly, it's kind of a cool outfit, but a bit depressing, no offence meant."

Matos Jason laughs, "None taken, and I was flying a mission. Into space, I think. I was assigned to… to… well that's bizarre, I can't remember. It was to do with rescuing people though, from somewhere. I wonder why I can't…"

"You know what else is strange?" Tavarez interrupts, "We can understand each other when we are speaking out loud. I understand it if I am in someone else's mind, but we are obviously not even from the same species, so how can we understand each other's languages?" Before Matos can answer, Tavarez continues with his questions. "If you don't remember what kind of mission, do you remember what kind of vehicle you were flying? A space shuttle? A faster-than-light spaceship? Of which we have neither on my world, sadly. That whole concept is just theories right now."

Matos Jason gives the young man a surprising answer, "No," he laughs, "I wasn't flying any of those. I was flying myself."

Tavarez stares directly into Matos Jason's eyes, confused by the response.

"I mean I can fly. You know, jump into the sky and fly by myself without assistance. Our world is full of beings with these marvellous abilities. Flight, speed, lots of other gifts. I was flying to, I guess wherever my mission was, but then this thing appeared and dragged me into it just as I saw the blackness start to swallow everything. I was helpless, totally helpless. I couldn't do anything." Matos Jason waves his hands and punches the air in frustration. "That same thing *rescued me* and then took me to you, before depositing us here."

"Wow, I am so sorry that happened to where you, wherever you are from. Now that I understand from that other me a little bit about multiple universes, it is kind of well, overwhelming and mind-bending, if you'll excuse the pun," Tavarez laughs a bit. "You can actually fly? Even in space? How do you do that? You can breathe up there? That's incredible!" Tavarez wonders if the seemingly-friendly alien was either joking with him, or was perhaps delusional. "Can you show me?"

"Of course! I can fly into space like that because I am somewhat indestructible."

Matos Jason thinks a leap into the sky would help clear his head and give him a chance to scout their surroundings with his far-sight from up above. He smiles at Tavarez, looks towards the sky and leaps straight up. Tavarez watches him make it a few feet into the air, and then fall right back onto the desert sands. "What the...? By the..."

Tavarez cannot make out the words but he guesses they are not polite ones.

Matos Jason tries flight a few more times, each one quickly ends with him back on the ground. Tavarez has trouble not laughing at the failed attempts, but not wanting to make things worse, does his best to look serious. When Matos Jason discovers his far-sight is not working either, he turns to his new friend and makes a strange request.

"Tavarez, can you hit me please? Hard."

Tavarez shakes his head in confusion, astounded by the request.

"It's okay, please, I need to check something. Just punch me in the stomach. It's important."

"Alright, if it's important but please don't punch me back," Tavarez wonders how much those large hands in the form of a fist would hurt. He does as he is asked, and then feels very bad when he hears Matos Jason groan.

"Ow! That really did hurt! Interesting! There must be power dampeners or something nearby. It is too bad I can't fly or I would be able to check things out from the air. Do you think this might be something that blackness is doing?"

Tavarez reflects, "I don't think so. I am pretty certain I would feel something if it was around or was the source that is interfering with your powers. I think it would be trying something like it did before, like getting into my mind if it was nearby."

Matos questions, "Okay, that's sort of comforting. Are you absolutely sure you saved your people? I mean how can you be so certain? Earlier you said something about multiple universes? What did you mean by that? I have heard our scientists theorize such a thing but nothing beyond that. How can you be so convinced of all this?"

"Um, if you will let me in, I can show you. I promise I will not be forceful, and I will just project, not search. I promise. I am learning very quickly now."

"Um sure, why not, go ahead. When you're done, you and I have a lot to talk about I guess."

When the telepathic knowledge transfer is done, Matos Jason understands why Tavarez believes his people safe and also how they were saved.

"Seems like this Devoid can be defeated, or at least driven away." Matos sounds hopeful.

"Yes, indeed it can," a Voice responds, startling them enough that they both jump. Matos Jason immediately assumed a defensive posture. "Much time to tell your stories. Very important you tell your stories to each other. Important indeed. You two have a long journey ahead of you. You have some very important people to meet once you get there, after all."

"Who are you? Get where?" Matos Jason is unnerved.

Even more so when Tavarez asks, "Why can't I read you? Did you speak out loud or into our minds? I couldn't tell, plus how can we both understand you or each other? Jason and I are not even from the same universes. Who are you?"

Matos adds, "Who are we supposed to meet and in what direction? And what have you done to my powers? Why won't they work here? Where are we?" he demands of the Voice.

"Oh my, sentients here, always full of so many questions! How exquisitely wonderful!"

The Voice ceases speaking. In the distance, though they both swear that they had not seen anything in any direction before, lies what looks like to Matos Jason, the outline of a spaceport. Tavarez sees the outline of an endless maze of mirrors. Assuming that each saw the same thing as the other, they silently begin walking towards its outline, far off in a distant horizon. At some point, Tavarez also realizes that though it appears to be day, there is no sign of any sun in the sky. Both now discuss this odd phenomenon before becoming quiet again, keeping their thoughts to themselves.

Eventually they become tired of the silence and begin to openly share their very different life stories, asking each other questions along the way. They laugh, cry and feel deeply as they unexpectedly come to know each other intimately, easily forging a bond of close friendship. So engrossed in their story telling, they do not notice hunger or thirst or have any sense of how long their journey is taking. Oddly enough, although they tell the stories of their lives in great detail, neither is able to remember the names of their home worlds.

A Guardian pleased. The Nexus anticipatory. The Devoid livid.
Two threads connected.

CHAPTER THREE

Quartet

In music, a quartet is an ensemble of four singers or instrumental performers, or a musical composition for four voices and instruments.

Tavarez and Matos Jason, feeling no weariness from their journey, draw closer to their destination. Tavarez still sees a largely constructed maze, while Matos Jason views a spaceport that is disturbingly quiet.

"We are almost there I think, the spaceport is a lot closer now," comments Matos Jason to his young new friend. "It is strange that it is so silent. No ships taking off or landing. I do wonder what that is about."

"The what? A spaceport? You mean the maze construct just ahead? It looks like it must have been built a long time ago, but I think I can see mirrors or reflections from it." Tavarez puts a hand over his eyes, attempting to block the glare from the mirrors so he can see the maze more clearly.

It seems impossible to see anything now and the look of confusion continues to grow more intense when Matos Jason speaks up, "You what? I don't understand, how can you not see the…wait, it's gone! How is that possible?" Matos Jason frowns in concentration, his hands waving before him as if trying to make the spaceport he saw rematerialize.

"So is the maze I was seeing! Some type of illusion maybe? What do you see now?"

"I think I see two life forms laying in the - is that grass?"

"Oh good, I see them too! At least we haven't lost our minds!"

"I'm not sure about that. Where did the sand go? When did we start walking on grass?"

"Mnnn," Matos Jason is contemplative. "At the moment, I am quite uncertain of that."

Lindsay and Bran sit in the shade of a tree near one of the pools, continuing their discussion. The sound of voices shocks them. They jump up to see two figures slowly approaching.

"Should we tell them to come closer?" Lindsay is concerned and asks her new friend.

"I think so," Bran confirms, "but just so you know, I am both frightened and glad to see other beings in this strange place."

"You are not alone in that." Lindsay watches the approaching pair, trying to make out anything that might look familiar; safe or dangerous.

"Welcome strangers," Bran gives a friendly gesture with his hand, palms up, as was the custom of his people when demonstrating peacefulness and nothing to fear to strangers.

"Thank you," responds the taller of the two. "Based on your appearances I would say you are both from different worlds, as are we, yet we can all understand each other. This a profound mystery indeed."

"Not just worlds, possibly even different universes," Tavarez reminds Matos Jason.

"What do you mean different universes?" Lindsay's curiosity is piqued. She examines the two newcomers more closely, marking their very different clothing, attesting to the idea that they are indeed from different worlds.

"Now that is a long tale, to be truthful, is it not Tavarez?" Matos Jason regards Tavarez closely, wondering if he might be of some help after all.

"Did you see the maze that was here earlier, or the spaceport?"

"No nothing like that!" Bran is surprised at the question and shakes his head, his colourful ponytail waving back and forth.

Lindsay speaks up, "Bran's right. Our first view of the place was most definitely not a maze or a spaceport. We actually came up through two different pools of water surrounded by this huge forest." She points, then looks completely astounded, her eyes blinking to confirm what she sees, or rather, what she does not see. "Oh my! The forest, the pools! They have vanished. It's all gone!" Only the grass they had been sitting on remained.

"When did that happen?" wonders Bran aloud, now thoroughly confused.

"I guess we were so busy telling each other our stories we completely missed whenever that happened. It was there! We swear it was! Even the pools we emerged from are gone, and there were so many! Way more than we could see, they just went on forever! And now they're gone along with the massive forest! It looked like it acted as some kind of barrier surrounding the pools, but maybe not?"

"Well, this is an odd place for certain!" exclaims Matos Jason. Thoughtfully he suggests, "Perhaps we should learn about each other, learn each other's stories? About where we are all from and how we all arrived here? After all, there doesn't seem to be much else to do at the moment. Maybe that will help us find some answers if we can find a common thread or a pattern in all our stories that helps solve this mystery."

The others nod in agreement.

"Makes sense to me," responds Bran.

Lindsay affirms, "Yes, why not? But Bran and I just finished doing that with each other. It's almost too bad we have to repeat everything again, but I guess that's the best we can do. Maybe one of you two could go first though since Bran and I just finished doing that?"

Hesitantly, Tavarez steps forward. "Um, I might be able to help with that. I mean, so you don't have to repeat everything."

"What do you mean?" Bran does not understand what Tavarez is implying.

"Tavarez, are you sure? It seems like it was all very new to you earlier." Matos Jason expresses his concern, although he anticipated this might come up as an option.

"It was, but I have a handle on it now. I have all the knowledge from the other version of me. I am very confident I can do this well, without any problem or violating anyone's boundaries."

"Okay, now you are scaring me a little," Lindsay continues, "and I am not even sure what you are talking about."

"I am a telepath," Tavarez announces proudly. "I can link all our minds together, so we can learn each other's stories much more quickly."

"Is that dangerous?" Bran echoes Lindsay's concern. "And what did you mean about the other version of yourself? I don't understand, do you have a twin?"

"Oh, that is complicated," Matos Jason laughs. "Tavarez might be right. His way might be the best. It won't take as long and I don't know why but I am feeling like there is some urgency with this."

"Urgency? For what?" Bran and Lindsay ask the questions together.

"Undetermined at this time," Matos Jason falls back into official investigative mode.

"Well, I am willing to try," says Lindsay. "At least Bran won't have to hear my whole sad tale all over again."

"I wouldn't mind anyway," Bran smiles, "It was an amazing thing to hear about your world. So different from mine. Sorry to hear it became so violent with all that death and destruction," he adds as an afterthought.

Lindsay wipes a tear away thinking to herself, *So much for doing anything significant now,* but saying out loud, "So how do we do this?"

Tavarez instructs the group, "I think it best if we all stand in a circle, hold hands, relax and think about our stories. Where we are from and how we arrived here, well, wherever we are. I promise, I will be gentle, slowly transferring images of your stories, your experiences from one to the other, until our whole group has shared together."

He continues, "I will share my story last," acknowledging to himself there are parts of his tale he prefers to keep private. "I promise to respect your privacy and boundaries. I will not pry into private thoughts or transfer any." He reflects momentarily, *Thank the Denizens I now have the skill and knowledge of how to do this thanks to the other Tavarez.*

"I think you will understand more, once I share my own story, which is why I will go last."

Seeing the group begin to a form a circle as he suggested, Tavarez steps in and holds Bran's hand on one side, and Lindsay's on the other. Matos Jason completes the loop by holding Lindsay's and Bran's free hands. Since the other three look both solemn and somewhat fearful, Tavarez attempts to reassure them, "Now just try to breathe slowly and relax. I will start gradually so this is not overwhelming for anyone. Bran would it be okay to start with you?"

Bran, always up for a new adventure agrees. "Sure, why not! Just be gentle please."

"Of course, now if you just slowly open your mind to me, I will learn your story and then transfer it in stages to the rest of the group. Is that okay?"

"Yes, actually this is kind of exciting, I think," Bran gulps, thinking maybe it wasn't the smartest move to volunteer first. He pushes that worry aside and does his best to relax. He feels the first twinges of an invading presence touch the fringes of his mind and then gradually enter in all the way, picking out his story. His sister, his mourning, his grief, his change of heart, the races, the fiery ocean, the collision, the fall into the boiling sea, his fear that he would die down there, the pool opening, the meeting with Lindsay and then it is over. No, not quite over, he can feel Tavarez now pushing the story from himself out to the others, all still linked together.

The process repeats with the other three, until lastly Tavarez shares his own journey with all the others. He is now proficient enough to connect with them all at once, so they receive his tale simultaneously, not individually as with the others' experiences. All of them see what Tavarez means by the other version of himself and they understand the danger that The Devoid presents.

So engrossed in the exchange of stories, eyes firmly shut, the group entirely misses the thick fog that develops and swirls around their circle and extends outwards from it for a good way during their telepathic interactions. Neither do they observe the fog lose its denseness, eventually turning into a light mist. Nor do they see the little girl that emerges from it.

At the end of their story sharing, eyes still closed in concentration, Bran shouts, "That is the same blackness I saw as I fell off my ship! By the Powers! What is that thing? That Devoid?"

"As you know now, I saw it too, just before I was pulled out of my universe," Jason Matos, opening his eyes, stares sadly at Bran, hoping The Devoid hadn't swallowed his universe too.

"But it can be defeated! You saw Tavarez's story and what his people were able to do, they pushed it back. Pushed it away. And it seemed like the other Tavarez was able to fight it too."

"I don't know how that helps us here though," Lindsay adds in. "Wherever here is? Does anyone know where we are yet anyway? I feel both lost and at home at the same time. It is such a weird feeling. Especially since I seem unable to remember the name of my home, the place I came from."

"I know what you mean. It's like I belong here, yet I don't. It's so odd." Bran expresses some of what they all are feeling, "I have the same problem. I can remember my story, just not the name of my world."

The others nod in solemn and surprised agreement, recognizing they too have the same challenge.

The four stay in the circle still holding hands, as though physical touch gives them comfort in this unknown place. They are so intently engaged in all they have seen and learned about each other, asking more questions and sharing intimately after such a powerful mental connection, they entirely miss the little barefoot girl with wavy, blond hair and bright smile, who has ducked underneath and between them and now stands in the centre of them.

When they finally become aware of her presence right in the midst of them, they all jump back in astonishment, releasing hands, breaking their formation.

"Oh my! Where did you come from, little one?" Matos Jason is perhaps more shocked than the rest. Normally he would have sensed the girl's presence long before she appeared.

"What is your name, little girl?" Lindsay is extremely curious, noting the girl had on the same type of gown that she wore, although of a different colour. Recognition dawns on her, a hospital gown! Now that is a strange coincidence!

"My name is Rebecca."

"That is a lovely name," Tavarez encourages her, while attempting to gently peer into the girl's mind, but without success. *"I have heard of those who are able to resist telepaths. I wonder if this is one of them or perhaps she is from a species that is naturally immune to such things,"* he thought and cautiously backs his mind probe away, asking out loud, "Do you have a last name, little girl?"

"Um, let me think, it's been so long and I have been walking for a very long time."

Bran encourages her, "Take your time. It appears we have lots of it here."

The little girl's brow furrows in concentration as though trying to remember what her last name might be. The quartet stares at her expectantly, but patiently. They sense it may be a long time before she responds.

CHAPTER FOUR

Quintet

A quintet is a group containing five members. It is commonly associated with musical groups, such as a string quintet, or a group of five singers, but can be applied to any situation where five similar or related objects are considered a single unit.

"Failsafe. That's it! My name is Rebecca Failsafe."

"Now I have a question for you," says the little barefoot girl with the wavy, blond hair and beautiful smile, her eyes aglow with the radiance of two miniature suns, staring intensely at each of them in turn, "What if you found the one true love that you had waited for all your life? And just when all seems so perfect, you discover that for them to live, in fact in order for everything you know and love to continue to be, you have to make the greatest sacrifice of all? You must give up everything, yourself, even them, for the sake of everything and everyone else to go on. Even for people places and things of which you know nothing? For universes and existences of which you have never ever even dreamed? But for their survival, it all depends on you? What if it was you on which everything else depended to survive? What if it was you? What if you were the Fifth Guardian?"

"Wow, that's a lot more questions than just one!" Lindsay expresses her surprise, mystified by this strange little girl.

"Big, deep questions to be coming from a little girl as young as you." Matos Jason wonders if this strange barefoot little girl with wavy blond hair who materialized out of nowhere can be trusted. Perhaps she is something more than what her appearance might lead one to believe. Then again, based on everyone's stories, all four of them appeared at their current location mysteriously too.

"What is a fifth guardian?" Tavarez is frustrated, for try as he might, gently or firmly, he cannot access the little girl's mind. He leans over, and whispers to Matos Jason, "I can't read her telepathically. She is either blocking me, or simply immune."

Upon hearing this Matos Jason's concerns raise a level, although his instincts tell him the girl is not dangerous, which totally confuses him. He reframes Tavarez's query and tries again. "Can you describe this fifth guardian?"

Rebecca smiles that beautiful smile that simply entrances Bran. "Well, like the other four, you know the ones right there," pointing in four different directions beyond the group. "I might say they are standing, but it really doesn't describe how they, how they," she struggles for words, and then straightens up, and says in a voice that sounds overlaid with another one, firm and authoritative, "How they manifest. Their appearances can be overwhelming for most sentients."

She smiles facing the four quite confused people she just met, all somewhat overwhelmed and unnerved by the change in her voice. Though she appears pleased and affirms to them, as much as to herself, announces, "You are the very, very important people..." She hesitates momentarily and corrects herself, "Very important person I am supposed to meet." She turns away from the group, looks up and points.

Four figures appear to the astonished group. Their forms bright and dense, more real perhaps than anything any of them have ever witnessed. Yet they intuitively understand even this manifestation is only for their benefit, this is not the true form or nature of the Guardians themselves, just something their finite minds are capable of absorbing.

"By The Powers!" exclaims Bran, completely overwhelmed with the sight. He falls to his knees, hands outstretched and lifted as though in worship.

"Holy! Are they? Is that?" Lindsay is uncertain what word to use, but ancient religious myths fill her mind.

Tavarez feels an unusual openness from the Guardians, a terrifying invitation, to enter into their thoughts. *"By the Denizens, what happens to me if I do that?"* and convinces himself he is not yet ready to take that step. Not right away at least.

Matos Jason maintains what he can of his professional demeanour, looking up at beings whose height dwarf anything in his experience and verbalizes what everyone else wants to ask. "What are you? Who are you?"

The beings remain silent, their stature and appearance more than enough to communicate their personage and power. The group looks on at immense beings arrayed in what some of their cultures would have considered military garb or some type of protective armour yet they wear no helmets or breastplates, but each of them is adorned with belts and scabbards obviously holding some fashion of swords within. A glowing coating covers their forms which the four sentients before them interpret as their apparel.

Lindsay, Bran, Tavarez and Matos Jason continue to stare, uncertain at what they are truly seeing. They remain speechless, unable to find words to match their awe. They look from Guardian to Guardian, faces of varying types and shapes form on each of them. The unique appearances expressed in such a manner, that one Guardian has a single face, another two faces looking in opposite directions, the third, three faces with one looking forward and two on either side, and the last, four faces, each positioned to see in a different direction. Their faces appear and disappear in an apparently random sequence, while the corporeal representations of the Guardians sometimes shift so that they are nearly transparent, the interiors of their beings filled with stars, galaxies, universes and other things indistinguishable.

Matos Jason thinks some of the faces are smiling, but steadies himself, reigns his thoughts in, and bravely asks, "How old are you? Who are you really?'

His questions directed both at the forms and the little girl, Matos Jason's senses are on full alert now. He is about to step closer to the little girl with the wavy blond hair to look her directly in her face, but hesitates, for in that moment The Voice speaks. The same Voice all of them heard at some point while here in this bizarre place.

"You are the Fifth Guardian," The Voice or was it Voices now, are not audible, but rather a soft almost melodious yet authoritative resonance within each of their minds.

Bran raises himself from his kneeling posture, the first to ask the question. Ignoring his almost overwhelming fear, with a false sense of bravado, he looks around and shouts verbally, "Which one of us is this Fifth Guardian?"

It is the question on all their minds, but he is the only one to verbalize it. "What do you mean? And which one of us do you refer to?"

The Voice or Voices, blend together, and repeat, "You are the Fifth Guardian," followed by an uncomfortable long silence.

Something tugs at Lindsay, a fleeting thought of insight and understanding she cannot fully complete. It has something to with what she just heard. The tug ceases; comprehension dawns. "Could that truly be what was meant?" Finally summoning up her courage, Lindsay speaks up, "Wait, do you mean all of us? As in plural, we all are the fifth guardian, whatever that is? Help us understand! Who are you?"

The Voices, definitely Voices this time, resound again. Then they realize, the Voice or Voices are coming from both Rebecca and something or somewhere else. If they listen closely, it is as though three voices are overlaid within each other but also separate and distinct, each with its own unique tone.

"Lindsay, your melody is always the desire to do something that will make a significant difference.

"Bran, having faced great tragedy, you understand deep loss and what it means to still move forward. Your melody resounds as an overcomer, regardless of the obstacles.

"Matos Jason, your powers mean you are the one who wants to save, not harm, to make things right, to rescue and help those in need, regardless of the sacrifice, notwithstanding what it may cost you. Whether you realize it or not, even without your powers, the desire to save at any cost would still be there, for yours is consistently the melody of a hero.

"And Tavarez, our dear Tavarez, so long have you struggled, questioned and yearned to be different, to be something more. You are! Your gift released has saved your people and your world. You now have the chance to put your gift to an unimagined use. Indeed, to be something different, to do something different. Your melody flows and resonates transformatively from hidden chords to an unfettered crescendo of something more, of someone who will save not just a world, but save multiple universes, indeed, to keep The All safe. To use your melody, to help restore Harmony. To correct The Balance."

The Voices turn their attention to the little eight-year-old barefoot girl with the wavy blond hair, bright, yellow eyes and glowing smile. "And you little one. You have travelled a long path and have at last returned home."

The other four watch the light of recognition dawn on the little girl's face as she nods in agreement.

"The unique rich melody bestowed upon you from long before your conception, was purposefully the opposite of all your other variations. It allowed you to bring hope and healing to the world of your birth. Now your tune will cause healing to spread on a much vaster scale across the entire All."

Rebecca Failsafe looks up, observing something unseen by the others, and speaks in a voice, crisp and clear, "Yes, the time is come."

Those watching her reaction to the Voice see the look of childhood innocence in her eyes mixed with wisdom incredibly ancient, well beyond her years. They struggle to understand the conversation and the meaning of everything that is occurring when The Voice addresses them directly.

"Our Potents! You were all chosen because of these destinies and desires.

Your passions, your melodies, can now reach their full potential. In true harmony you will become *The Fifth Guardian!*"

The title echoes loudly, and the group trembles.

"Behold," although The Voices may have been mistaken for audible this time, they are not. Rather now within their minds, just as Tavarez had been not that long ago. In their mind's eye they begin to see the song of the Guardians unfold from before the dawn of known creation, as the fundamental primal forces of Time, Space, Eternity and Infinity take shape.

Their origins, their roles, their part, their guardianship, how it was bestowed, how it came to pass was made clear. They see worlds, galaxies, universes and all their iterations and variations across the vast span of time, unfolding, folding, living, dying, repeating. Beings, species, ancient and present, the whole story of untold eons fills their thoughts. It is so much, yet they understand it and in a nanosecond all becomes clear.

Very clear too, is the darkness, the struggle against the emptiness, the understanding of chaos and order and what lurks behind it. They observe the timelines ruined, maladjusted, bent and twisted. Destinies corrupted, they see and understand both the eventual and the imminent danger, the collapse of all things into an everlasting blackness of nothingness. They witness their counterparts from other times and places across The All, comprehend their fates, the choices, the tricks of influence that had negated their variations from being in this place, but had led them here, the surviving Potents.

It is as if Tavarez has been prepared for this precise moment. Right now. He understands that if his gift had activated when younger, he might have missed the connection with his other version. He might not have learned of The Devoid, nor saved his world or even his universe. There is a reason. His destiny brought him to this place. This is why the gift finally manifested after all those years of pain, fear and prejudice. The timing was not right before. So simple. Yet so profound.

He smiles. More so than the others, he realizes he can withstand the onslaught of information and rapidly changing pictures, the history of everything. Of The All. Instinctively he begins reaching out to the other three, supplementing and strengthening their minds, holding them together as one. He finds a piece of the little girl's mind open for him as well. He reaches out, gently, finds what he seeks, and now understands her. What she is. Who she is. Why she is here now. That is more than enough. He gently transmits this new knowledge to the other three. The words come again, softer and more musical than before.

"You are the Fifth Guardian."

The Fifth Guardian

FINALE

A finale is the last <u>movement</u> of a <u>sonata</u>, <u>symphony</u>, or <u>concerto</u>; the ending of a piece of non-vocal <u>classical music</u> which has several movements; or, a prolonged final sequence at the end of an act of an <u>opera</u> or work of <u>musical theatre.</u>

Lindsay, Bran, Tavarez and Matos Jason start holding hands again without realizing it. This time Rebecca Failsafe joins in, holding hands within their circle. They now comprehend her role as well. They stand staring at each other, wondering what comes next. The weight of their collective anticipation is nigh unbearable.

The brilliance is blinding. The five individuals gaze in awe at what surrounds them. Portals, doorways, space, time, light, dark, infinity, eternity, destiny, all begin to be quite comprehensible in their evolving state. Their heads begin to throb in pain. One holds his stomach, feeling an overwhelming urge to vomit in response to the unending motion his corporeal system is now unable to deal with.

Intuitively there is an understanding of what must be done. This is not something to be accomplished by a solo effort. They experienced a very brief foretaste of it when Tavarez linked their minds. The sharing of stories was one thing, it was necessary; a prelude of what was to come. But this is different. Very different.

Lindsay feels it first. The sifting. The changing. The melding. The union of beings. She feels the force of a dynamo tearing her apart and putting her back together. She is unmade, remade and reshaped. There is light such as she has never seen before and the gift of a new type of vision. Vision so wide, she cannot immediately adjust. A perspective previously unknown and unreachable now flooding her new heightened cosmic senses.

Now infinity, eternity, space, time and destiny, come in and out of focus in rapid succession. Then come into focus again. She feels the others now, the lightness of being, merging consciousnesses, memories, pain, suffering, joy, five lifetimes combined into one new state of being, of untethered consciousness, now feeling more control, now less, striving for dominance, then relenting and surrendering. She wonders if the others are feeling the same, but realizes she does not need to wonder, she knows they are.

Then, slowly at first, a grip on reality, a feeling of control, then spiralling down, moving slowly, centring now, she sees "herself" through the whirlwind of chaos, through the blurring of the senses, narrowing down to a single place on a single planet in a single solar system, in a single galaxy, in a single universe, past all, she sees Lindsay, a different version of herself. Tears stream down her new face in joy, bewilderment and comprehension. She rejoices that she, or at least this Lindsay, is safe.

They all experience something similar, including the tears. Other versions of themselves along with those they know and love, still in existence across The All. Loving, Laughing, Playing. All of them safe. A sense of overwhelming relief. Even understanding those they see are different than those they knew before, still inspires hope. The Voice speaks. Clearly. Intensely. Urgently into their minds, *"Safe for now, but it will not be so without the Fifth Guardian. You are the Fifth Guardian."*

Jason Matos feels the tear in the fabric of his being. It is being shredded into millions of splinters, divided and subdivided, it hurts, yet does not hurt, feeling somehow wonderful and painful simultaneously. Life and death, beginning and ending intertwined, losing himself, then regaining himself, weakness like death, strength never felt before, even for him.

Then the merging and meshing, the joining of five individual beings, including him, into something different, something unique, something better. He does not lose himself though, he becomes more than he ever thought possible. First a sense of overwhelming chaos and then order.

Bran feels the terrible urge to throw up. This is not what he expects. The motion, the spinning, is deadly. Then he feels his physical body beginning to give way, his physical shell transforming, his consciousness no longer tethered to physicality in the same way. A dizzying maelstrom of exhilaration and terror combined. His merging, emotions swelling, his being melding, not losing itself, but growing stronger than he ever imagined, becoming something different. His vision grows so broad, so huge, so large, eyes burning, if they were still eyes, it is hard to tell. He is lost in space, time, eternity, infinity, destiny, he sees the light, the black, senses the darkness that wishes to push itself into the portals, through the gateways. but he also sees it receding. He sees schisms and splits being sealed, as he feels strength grow within this merger of beings.

It is as though the more the merging evolves, the more the darkness recedes and is forced out, having a foothold no longer. It is moving back, outside of all existence and he sees it and more. He knows the challenge is not over yet - it is just beginning.

The light of a billion suns cascade through the little barefoot girl with the wavy blond hair and radiant smile. The sensations are overwhelming to her mortal body. Powerful, fearful but not unfamiliar. A mixture of suffering and relief until all is momentarily quiet. Peaceful. Then suddenly she bubbles up with feelings, emotions, memories, on top of each other piled high, in rapid succession, filling, overwhelming, building, tears, laughter, everything from four other lives, driving hard, filling, emptying and filling again. It is not too much for her; she possesses that little part of the Nexus to sustain her. She is the anchor, the centrepiece holding them all together. Her mission is almost complete. She is the Failsafe. It is time.

Tavarez focuses. He feels it all and more importantly, comprehends the blackness, the Devoid. He sees it, sees the tendrils receding, sees the outside of all places where timelines reasserted themselves, worlds where true destinies were now grasped willingly and this time not averted or misaligned by odd twists and turns the darkness caused in its lust to destroy and deceive.

He sees it…they all observe it…together…it has more meaning for him perhaps, but they all feel what he feels. They see the other Four Guardians now in their true form. The same form they now possess. Their being now linking and interacting with the others. The other Guardians watching remember now how they came to be, how their origins occurred, how they manifested, how they were created. It is refreshing to remember.

The Four Guardians reach out and welcome the Fifth. A new merging and meshing occurs as all five together share a common understanding of Eternity, Infinity, Space, Time and Destiny together. They learn. They believe. They understand. They know what must be done to defeat The Devoid. They need no words. No instruction. No direction. Their task clear. The Fifth Guardian come into its own.

They feel the sheer force of their combined wills in place, driving back the malevolence that had hid itself behind chaos. Its mask now unveiled. No longer undetectable. The damage that had been done can not be undone. What has been lost, can not be unlost. The gateways and portals that closed, the pools that dried up, will remain that way now. But the cracks, the fissures, the breaches begin to seal.

The combined wills of the new Fifth Guardian now join with the other Four, attainability strong and growing stronger. The darkness is being forced back and receding. The Five Guardians are fencing it in, forcing it to release any holds. They attack it directly, hitting all its forms, wrapping themselves in the unbearable light of the Unending, supplemented by the new addition of the Fifth, overpowering the darkness, shredding it into nothingness.

Their powerful wave travels through every planet, solar system, galaxy, universe and dimension, laying all aspects of The Devoid bare, burning away all tendrils, dissolving any and every remnant of the creature.

The Devoid is caught unawares, not expecting this frontal assault. It first feels Its tendrils spread out across The All catch on fire and burn with the heat of innumerable stars. It feels the searing flames spread, dematerializing portions of Itself. Ones both visible and ones It kept hidden. The agony is unbearable.

It is furious as well. It is so close to locating the Nexus, but to no avail. It attempts to hide itself, but the Guardians will have none of it. They are relentless in their attack. Five immovable, unstoppable wills cascading in energies beyond what even The Devoid can absorb. There is no relief. It struggles as Its own sentience begins to drift away as they attack Its core. Right in the centre of Its being, Its will, Its mind, is no match for the onslaught. It despairs as the Five Guardians' light seeks out all Its parts, every piece of It throughout The All, and negates whatever they can find of the creature into oblivion. Nowhere to hide.

Its foes continue to wreak their punishment, unleashing it in a steady torrent. The Guardians now summon the unlimited powers of Eternity, Time, Space and Infinity to their aid. Fashioning aspects of those fundamental forces into weapons, they mercilessly target all that is left of the Devoid, with no quarter given. A sustained crescendo of unrelenting power is tearing the Devoid apart. It is the Devoid's finale.

There is no denying it. The Devoid knows it. The battle is lost. Its opponents will allow no surrender. Show no mercy. They will tolerate nothing but Its utter destruction. A final, refreshed primal force comes into play, revitalized and refreshed from the birth of the New Guardian. Destiny. Destiny has endured enough of being trifled with by this creature. Of being twisted, subsumed, abrogated, misaligned and misdirected. Destiny. This newly reinvigorated force bursts forth with a vengeance. Vengeance on behalf of all the sentients whose destinies The Devoid had corrupted. Destiny pummels and punches directly into the remaining bits of The Devoid's unholy core with a fury unparalleled. An uncompromising retribution that not even The Devoid with all Its dark will, is able to match or master, causing the creature's very essence to finally, completely rupture in dreadful agony.

The Devoid is angry but no longer has the wherewithal to focus it, to use it, to bring it to bear. It has no energy to summon or create the havoc that has been Its trademark. It has nothing left but Its own blackness. All Its dark emotional energies siphoned over millennia that had coalesced and eventually brought it into being are rapidly dissipating. Its fate is sealed. With a last barrage from the Five Guardians, all remnants of It across The All vanish, melting away into nonexistence.

The healing across The All will not be immediate. This is only the beginning. It will take more than just centuries, for it will be eons for things to ultimately right themselves, but this is a start. The recovery has begun. The timelines, the appointed destinies, will find their way to stability. The intersections will connect at the right times in the right places. The barriers will solidify the pillars. Slowly but eventually, the vastness of The All will find balance. From Points of Origin to every iteration, the cracks will mend. A new song. The Symphony will continue.

Infinity. Space. Time. Eternity. Destiny.

All reestablished, adjusted, revitalized, refreshed, restored.

The Symphony that is The All, playing out Melody and Harmony in perfect balance and rhythm. Once more.

The Fifth Guardian assumes their place.

The Four resume their Guardianship.

The Fifth positions itself in the Nexus at the centre of the Four.

Five Guardians always ready.

Over the portal underneath.

Within and Without.

The Devoid defeated.

For now.

Sacrifices made.

Breaches closed.

The All healing.

The Nexus safe.

All realities mending.

The Sentinels complete.

Guardians of Space, Time, Infinity, Eternity, Destiny.

The Fifth Guardian holds in the appointed place.

Postlude

Postlude is the lesser-known counterpart to "prelude" - and in fact, "postlude" was created based on the example of "prelude," substituting "post-" for "pre-." At the root of both terms is the Latin verb ludere ("to play"), and a postlude is essentially "something played afterward."

The young mer-teen swims through the watery depths.

He has been swimming for a long time.

Yet he is not hungry or thirsty.

He does not understand why.

He just is not.

He keeps swimming.

ACKNOWLEDGEMENTS

Iwould like to acknowledge the patience of my lovely wife Beth as I worked on this story that has been a long time in coming to fruition. She is truly my inspiration, and my encourager. Additionally I owe a great debt of gratitude to my editor/cover art designer/coach, Paula Telizyn for her editorial input and excellent suggestions as well as my proofreader, Shannon Carroll Wiedener. Their diligent work and attention to detail was invaluable in helping to ensure the story is at a level of excellence that readers will appreciate. I would also like to recognize the many people I have known personally over the years who have endured unexpected tragedy and loss, and kept going despite the challenges and the absence of an answer to the often asked, "Why?" Their faith, fortitude and perseverance are truly something to behold and treasure. This story is to acknowledge them and others who share similar life experiences. Perhaps they are the real Guardians.

About the Author

Barry M. Fellinger resides in St. Thomas Ontario with his wife Beth and. He enjoys spending time with his children and grandchildren, extended family, and friends. He also likes reading books from a variety of genres, watching superhero and science fiction television shows and movies, collecting comics, attending the occasional Comicon and relaxing in Sanctuary II, his comic book/man room for inspiration.

He has authored two sci-fi adventure books in his True Adventure Series for middle grade readers, The Almost True Adventures of Brandon and Josh and its sequel The Not So True Adventures of Brandon, Josh and Adam. Both books are available through online distributors in e-book and paperback formats. The first book in the series, The Almost True Adventure of Brandon and Josh is also now available as an audiobook.

For more information on Barry and his books where you will find updates on Barry's writing activities as well as his video series about Sheepy Weepy Wimpy Wompy, now called the Town of Meh, , please visit www.barrymfellingerauthor.com